A MURDER IN HELVETICA BOLD

Thistlewood Star Mystery #1

C. RYSA WALKER

STARRY NIGHT BOOKS

☆ Chapter One ☆

I HELD MY BREATH, pointing the binoculars toward the tiny flash of yellow-orange. A golden-crowned kinglet, maybe? It would help to have a picture to compare later with ones online, and I mentally cursed myself for not investing in binoculars with a built-in camera. This pair had been a spur-of-the-moment purchase, though. I patted my pockets for my phone to take a picture before remembering that it was in my purse and most likely dead. Back in Nashville, the thing had been practically glued to my hand. I was surprised how little I'd used it since coming back to Thistlewood.

Okay, then, I thought. *Birdwatching is supposed to be about living in the moment. I'll just watch the little guy. You don't have classify everything you see, Ruth. Just breathe deep. Enjoy the morning.*

Despite the slight chill, that was an easy thing to do. I've always loved this time of year, when the trees begin dressing themselves for spring, with tiny, wistful buds of green popping up here and there. I just hoped they weren't being too optimistic. Like most mountain villages, Thistlewood has been known to get a killing frost in early spring. But after a long, hard winter, maybe a bit of optimism was in order.

And it *had* been a long, hard winter, not just for the trees, but for me. The slower pace had been a good thing, all in all. After leaving Nashville, I'd needed some time to heal. To find out exactly who I was and what I wanted.

Thinking about Nashville still brought a hitch to my throat. Not tears, like it had for the first few months, but more of a bittersweet feeling—warmth, nostalgia, and just a touch of anger and regret. I'd had a life there. A good one, I'd thought. But that was water under the bridge—nine months and one husband ago. At forty-nine, on the razor's edge of fifty, Ruth Townsend was starting over.

Something warm and furry joined me on top of the picnic table wedged into the corner of my small deck. Cronkite, who everyone says must be at least part Maine coon cat given his size, usually came out with me first thing. He likes to bird-watch, too, although I suspect it's for an entirely different reason.

This morning, however, Cronkite had been curled up in bed with my daughter, Cassie, who was visiting for the week. I figured I had another minute, tops, before he swatted at my binoculars to remind me that breakfast had not yet been served. So I shifted slightly to the left and leaned forward across the railing to get a better look at my feathered friend.

But it was too late. Cronkite must have spotted the bird, too, because he let out a throaty yowl. The little bird took wing, disappearing into the faint rays of orange and gold spilling across the tops of the eastern mountains.

I lowered the binoculars. "You scared him away, Cronk." I expected him to respond with his usual air of self-satisfaction. But when I looked down at the cat, his gray-and-white coat was standing on end, as if he'd taken a bath with the toaster. And he wasn't staring at the spot where the bird had been. His eyes were fixed on an entirely different location at the edge of the woods.

Now I could hear it, too. There was a crackle of underbrush, and then a black bear came bounding into the backyard. My breath caught, and I froze, hoping not to startle him. The bear—no longer a cub but not fully grown, either—looked up, and our eyes met.

Remy. I smiled down at him. *You're back.*

The bear, who had gained at least thirty pounds during the past five months, turned his head sideways, examining me every bit as much as I was examining him. Was he thinking that I'd added some weight over the winter, too?

Cronkite, in his official role as guard cat, hissed a warning.

"Shh. It's just Remy. You'll scare him off."

Cronk ignored me and hissed again, although he seemed a bit less certain about his authority now than he'd been back in November, when his weight and the cub's had been roughly on par. Remy never made it onto Cronkite's very short list of approved visitors, despite spending the better part of a week as a guest in our shed. I'd actually thought the cub was a large rat when I saw him the first time, huddled in a back corner. That's why I named him after the main character in the movie, *Ratatouille*.

On closer inspection, I'd discovered that my intruder was not, in fact, a giant rodent, and that his leg was caught in a piece of concertina wire some fool had left in the woods. Remy was about the size of a poodle back then, and I'd been worried he'd bite if I tried to untangle him. I'd called the local vet and left a message, since she was out. Then I'd bundled up in several layers of winter coats to protect my arms, topped off with barbecue gloves that came clear to my elbows, and went back out to see what I could do. Remy seemed to sense that I was trying to help, and while he winced and whined a few times, he never once snarled.

The vet had finally shown up a few hours after his leg was free. She applied some antiseptic but said that the only thing to do at that point was to stock that corner of the shed with food and water and leave the door open so that the little guy could leave when he was ready. Each time I went out to check on him, I was constantly looking over my shoulder, terrified that the mama bear was going to come crashing out of the woods, assuming I was the one who'd hurt her cub and, as I'd eventually discovered, killed her mate. Even though I'd learned online that black bears never attack in defense of their cubs—that's a brown and grizzly bear trait—I was still on edge. There's an exception to every rule. What if I'd stumbled upon the one black bear cub with a stereotypical angry mama?

And Mama Bear *was* watching. I'd seen her a few times from the kitchen window, keeping a close eye on the shed. But she never approached. Remy's leg healed steadily, and he proved himself to be a bit of a clown when I stopped by the shed to check on him. Then, one morning, I'd awakened to find him gone. This was the first I'd seen of him since then.

I'd been a little worried about him during the long winter months. That was kind of silly, I guess. From everything I'd read, he'd been cozied up inside a cave with his mama, sleeping in until spring.

The bear was still watching me. Maybe he was looking for food? I hated the idea that he might be hungry and was torn between tossing him something and the knowledge that it's never wise to feed the bears. Remy might not hurt me, but he could easily have friends and family out there.

A third, much louder hiss from Cronkite finally broke through the bear's trance. Remy's head jerked toward the cat, then he slashed back into the under-brush and disappeared.

"Way to go, Cronk. Are you proud?"

Cronkite *did* look quite pleased with himself. He

pushed through his cat door, marched to his bowl, and stared directly at me.

"Right. Breakfast. I'm on it."

As I opened the cat food, I looked out the windows to see if Remy was still lurking in the underbrush. But he was gone. I kind of hoped he'd stop by again sometime, but I was also glad my deck was a good fifteen feet up from the gently sloping ground below. Maybe it would be best if Remy stuck to the woods. It had been nice to see him, though. Nice to know that we'd both survived the long winter.

I glanced down at my watch. Six thirty on the dot. The temperature was still in the lower forties. Not exactly freezing but not parade-around-in-your-skivvies weather, either. I took a sip from my coffee—now tepid, just the way I like it—and stashed my binoculars in the hall closet. Those newspapers weren't going to deliver themselves.

The Thistlewood Star has been the town's weekly newspaper for generations. I began helping Mr. Dealey set the type when I was thirteen, long before he could legally put me on the payroll. Instead, I was paid in books. New books, used books, even comic books. When I got to high school, my English teacher, Lucy McBride, urged me to work on the school paper, but it was little more than a gossip column. Instead, I continued at the *Star*, where Mr. Dealey let me do some actual reporting. By the time I left for college, I had nearly five years of newspaper experience, something few incoming freshmen could claim.

Mr. Dealey continued running the *Star* on his own until he died five years ago. The paper had always hovered on the edge of being profitable, and the equipment was so antiquated that few people knew how to use it. As a result, the presses literally stopped when Mr. Dealey died. My goal since returning to Thistlewood has been to get the paper back on its feet. It will never make me rich, but between what my parents left me when they died—this house and a modest savings account—and my early retirement from the *News-Journal*, I really only needed the paper not to *lose* money for very long.

And, at some point, I hope the paper becomes profitable enough for me to hire a kid to do the deliveries, and maybe even teach her or him to set the type or write a few stories, like Mr. Dealey did with me. It would be nice to pay it forward. But when that day comes, I suspect I'll miss walking the route, stopping to chat with subscribers as they head off to work, and sometimes even stumbling upon an idea for a story.

Reviving the *Star* had been slow going, but I *was* making progress. As of the previous Friday, when I'd received two new subscriptions, my regular readership now officially numbered in the dozens. Twenty-four subscribers and nearly fifty additional copies sold at local stores. Not too shabby for two months' work.

What we need is a good mystery, I thought as I stood up. *Something to get the tongues wagging and the papers flying off the shelves.* Of course, in a sleepy little town like Thistlewood, that was about as likely as snow on a clear August day.

After I fed Cronk and rinsed out my coffee mug, I began looking for my cell phone. Service is crappy at best in most parts of town. If you want to get in touch with someone, it's often better to hang out at Pat's Diner. Most people stop in there on a daily basis during the off-season. Even during the summer when the town is flooded with tourists, we'll often drop by for takeout if the line isn't out the door. The food is decent, and the place has a classic 1950s diner vibe, with red leather booths, personal jukeboxes at your table, and framed vintage photos that I'd assumed were stock photography until one day when the owner's mom had been in a particularly chatty mood. She spent the better part of an hour telling me which Thistlewood citizens—past and present, almost none of whom I knew—were in the pictures.

My phone finally turned up at the bottom of my purse and, as I'd suspected, was dead as the proverbial doornail. I stashed the phone back in my purse along with a charging cable and was almost to the front door when a voice called out from the staircase, startling me so badly that my heart jumped track.

"Good grief, Cassie! You scared the heck out of me."

"Well, good morning to you, too, Mom." She grinned, running a hand through her tangled mass of short dark curls. Those curls are one of the things she inherited from me, although mine lacked the deep purple highlights Cassie was currently sporting. I'd learned not to get too attached to any particular shade where my daughter was concerned. The colors changed like the wind.

"Just didn't hear you come down, that's all."

While I'd grown accustomed to it just being me and Cronkite in the mornings, it had been really nice having Cassie home for the past few days. The house was going to feel empty when she went back to Nashville. Her work kept her there most of the time, and it was nearly a four-hour drive. But the distance had a silver lining, too. We'd both been taking each other for granted a bit. I hadn't fully appreciated the luxury of being able to see her anytime I wanted. Now, on weeks like this one, when she had time off and was able to make it down for a visit, we made the most of every moment.

She sat on the bottom step with her arms clasped around her knees. "Where are you headed?"

"I have papers to deliver. The citizens of Thistle-wood must have their breaking news."

She rolled her eyes. "Breaking news in Thistlewood is someone's dog jumping the fence."

"Occasionally," I said. "But we can't take that much excitement *every* week. Best to stick to things like the monthly town council meeting and whatever new items Pat adds to the menu at the diner."

"Be still, my beating heart. You don't need to bother with the papers, though. I made your deliveries after I picked them up from the printer."

"All of them? Last night? Where did you get the addresses?"

She snorted. "You're kidding, right? You have that list on the front desk. Or maybe I should call it a shrine. *Eternal Thanks to Our Beloved Subscribers.*"

I laughed. "It does *not* say that."

"Anyway, it took me a half hour, tops. It would have been even less if not for that one house out in the boonies."

"Well, thank you," I said, trying to keep the slight note of disappointment out of my voice. I appreciated the gesture, but I also kind of enjoyed my early-morning delivery walks. That wasn't so true in the dead of winter, but the weather was nice this morning.

"Consider it an early birthday present," Cassie said. "Is there coffee?"

I placed my purse back on the small table by the door. "Yes. But it's cold by now. I'll make a fresh pot."

Cronkite had just settled into his corner by the sliding door, no doubt checking to be certain Remy the Wonder Cub didn't wander onto his turf again.

"We had a visitor this morning," I said to Cassie. "Remember the bear cub I told you about? I spotted him while I was out on the deck."

Cassie glanced out the door. "Is that normal this time of year?"

I shrugged. "I'm not sure. I was glad to see he wasn't limping. Looks like he didn't suffer any perma-nent damage from the injury."

"Did you get a picture this time?"

"No," I said. "Didn't even think about it. Besides, my phone is dead."

"Again?" Cassie kneeled down and scratched Cronkite behind the ears. "Good thing you were here, boy. Protecting the house like a big brave kitty."

"Oh, he did his job, all right. Scared the poor little guy right back into the woods. So, what's on your agenda for today?"

"I don't know. Probably hang out here for a while and then stop by the library. If I'm going to be here for a whole week, I'll need something to read."

"You don't have to stay your *entire* vacation, you know. I do understand if you have more exciting things to do than hang out with your mom in Thistlewood."

"It's not such a bad place," she said. "A little tame in the winter, but I had a lot of fun when I used to visit in the summer. And you can't get rid of me that easily. I want to be here for your birthday."

"Ugh." I finished putting the coffee on and left the machine to do its work. "No one wants to be reminded that she's turning fifty. You get enough of a reminder simply looking in the mirror."

"Yep, fifty is *so* old," Cassie said with a grin. "But getting old is better than the alternative, right? And you're still beautiful. I'm not the only one who thinks so, either. I saw the way Ed Shelton looked at you last night."

I rolled my eyes. Ed and I had been hanging out together for a few months, but it wasn't anything romantic. While I wouldn't be averse to that at some point, I wasn't ready to plunge back down *that* particular rabbit hole just yet. Cassie and I had gone to Pat's for dinner the night before, and Ed had stopped by to chat for a bit, but as far as I could tell, he hadn't looked at me any differently than usual. Or any differently than he looked at anyone else.

My daughter has always been observant, though. She picks up on people's moods and can spot a lie at fifty yards. Cassie would have made a brilliant reporter if she'd ever had the inclination.

That said, I could tell from the gleam in her eye that she was trying to figure out how to play matchmaker, and I didn't intend to give her anything to play with. "You have an overactive imagination, Cassie. Ed and I are just friends."

"How long have you known him?" she asked, not even acknowledging my comment. "And why haven't you told me a single thing about him?"

"Ed grew up in Thistlewood. He's a bit older than me, but I knew his younger sisters."

I ignored her last question, even though it was a very perceptive one. The truth is, I really didn't know how to answer. Cassie and I talked a few times a week. I'd told her lots of stories about Wren and some of the other people I knew in town. The fact that I hadn't mentioned Ed yet suggested that maybe some part of my brain *had* been thinking of him in a romantic way all along. Not that I really thought Cassie would object, but the divorce from her father had only been final for a few months. Ed had stopped by to chat almost every day since I opened up the newspaper. I'd even had lunch with him at Pat's a couple of times and gone to a few poker games that he and some of his ex-cop or former military buddies held every two weeks or so. He'd never pitched it as a date, just a way of introducing me (or in some cases, reintroducing me) to people in the area.

But I hadn't said a peep about any of that to Cassie.

"He used to be the sheriff," I continued. "So I knew *of* him even if I didn't really know him, mostly from my subscription to the *Star* when I was in Nashville. The sheriff plays a leading role in any small-town paper. And, of course, his accident made the news, even in Nashville. Not front page, but a sheriff getting sideswiped on the side of the road merits at least a mention."

"So that's what happened," Cassie said. "I noticed the limp but didn't want to ask."

"Yeah. It was New Year's Eve, seven years ago. Just a routine traffic stop. Ed was standing on the shoulder of the road. Whoever hit him was almost certainly drunk, judging from the way they were swerving. He saw part of the license plate and the make and model, but the owner, who was still in high school, had a decent alibi and a powerful grandfather. That kid's dad is the sheriff now, in fact, and the boy still drives like a maniac, so you might want to keep a watch out if you're downtown late at night."

A burp and hiss from the kitchen told me that the

coffee was finished brewing. I poured myself a travel mug and headed for the door.

"You're still going in?" Cassie asked with a fake pout.

"Yes, but only a half day. I need to deliver copies to the diner and to the stores that carry them. And I'm still working on getting the press up and running so that we don't have to go all the way to Knoxville each week."

"I can't believe you're still able to get parts for it," Cassie said. "And the drive into Knoxville would take a lot less time than using that ancient monstrosity."

"You can still special order the parts," I replied a little defensively. "And don't talk that way about Stella. She was my baby long before you came along."

To be fair, though, Cassie was right. Although there had been some minor updates, the printing press, which Mr. Dealey nicknamed Stella, was the same machine that had been used at the *Star* since it opened in the early 1900s. And yes, it would be much quicker to continue having the paper printed in Knoxville. Much easier, too, but it's definitely not cheaper. And it just didn't feel the same.

"Anyway," I told her, "the press is part of the attraction. I'm hoping we can get tourists to stop in, since Stella is one of only a few old-fashioned printing presses in the nation."

Cassie looked skeptical. "Isn't that a lot of effort just to sell a few extra papers?"

"Maybe. But it could also help draw business to the shops on my block. I'm being a good corporate citizen."

She laughed. "You just don't like change."

"Not true," I said as I opened the door. "I simply believe you need to balance the old with the new. Have fun today! Maybe drop by the paper after you're done at the library." I paused as I was about to close the door. "But I won't be there at lunch."

"Going on a date?" Cassie wagged her eyebrows at me.

"Yes. With Wren. She told me you're welcome to join us if you'd like."

Cassie wrinkled her nose. "Are you having lunch at her *house*?"

Wren Lawson, my best friend for as long as I can remember, owns the Memory Grove Funeral Parlor in Thistlewood. She lives above the chapel and mortuary, something that freaks Cassie out more than a little bit. Wren is a pragmatic soul, who has always viewed death as simply another stop in the circle of life. Cassie, on the other hand, goes out of her way to avoid walking past a graveyard or funeral home.

"Yes. At her house. She has something she wants to give me. Although I could probably convince her to meet us at the diner if it means she'd get to see you, too."

"Oh, that's okay," Cassie said. "Don't worry about me. I'll just make a salad when I get back. We ate at the diner last night, and I don't want to mess up your plans."

"You know, if you went to Wren's house just once, you'd see it's really not a big deal," I said gently. "I mean, we're *all* going to end up in a place like Memory Grove eventually."

"Working there, I can understand," she says. "Okay, not really. That's not a job I would ever take. But *living* there? No way."

"You live above a magic shop. Some people might think *that's* strange."

Cassie groaned. "Nirvana is *not* a magic shop. It's a metaphysical bookstore."

"It's a new-agey place. The sign always makes me think of witches and crystal balls."

"We sell *crystals*, Mom. Not crystal balls." Cassie dumped a spoonful of sugar into her cup.

"You also sell those chakra thingies," I added. "Plus tarot cards. And what about the psychic who comes in to give readings each weekend? It's a magic shop."

"Fine," she said with a laugh. "Call it whatever you want. But it's not even remotely as bizarre as living above a funeral home."

☆ Chapter Two ☆

LIKE MOST SMALL TOWNS, Thistlewood's Main Street is its lifeline. Almost everything is located off the two-lane blacktop. Pat's Diner is at one end, and a large church at the other. In between, you have an assortment of small shops, many of which are closed in the winter, along with the courthouse, the library, a small movie theater that's shuttered during the winter, another church, the drugstore, and the offices of the *Thistlewood Star.* This is the core of the town, the part that existed before the tourist attractions began to spring up around the river and the gateway to the Smoky Mountains National Park. During the off-season, the townsfolk seem to cluster around this narrow strip, which everyone thinks of as the *real* Thistlewood. I guess we're a bit like bears in the winter, and Main Street is the communal cave in which we gather to hibernate.

Thistlewood's winters are always tough. We aren't high up enough for skiing, and the town lacks the flashy allure of nearby Pigeon Forge or Gatlinburg. There used to be two local factories, but pretty much all we have now is the river. In warmer weather, the cabins and campgrounds are filled with families who spend their vacation days fishing, swimming, or inner-tubing. It also doesn't hurt that the casinos at Cherokee are only a short drive away.

Back when I was in high school, the town went into snooze mode after Halloween. We'd get hunters and a few of the more diehard fishermen in the late autumn months, but they didn't buy much aside from food at the diner. In recent years, though, some smart cookie on the town council came up with the idea of turning Thistlewood into a picture-perfect Christmas village. It took a while to catch on, but the gimmick has done a decent job of drawing visitors from Knoxville, Asheville, even as far away as Chattanooga, to buy knickknacks and handmade goods for the holiday season. But from January to mid-March, the town remains a veritable graveyard.

I'd forgotten exactly how dead the place could be during the thirty years I was away. It was one of those not-entirely-relevant things that you stash away at the back of your head. Because I'd never planned on returning to Thistlewood for more than a few days at a time. My career and my life were both in Nashville.

But things change, and sometimes they change wicked fast. When the paper I'd worked at for nearly twenty-five years was bought out by one of those big syndicates, they offered several of the writers and editors an early retirement package. At first, I resisted the idea. I liked my job, and I was too young to retire. But my friend Wren had reminded me that there was nothing wrong with retiring from one job and moving on to new adventures. My husband, Joe, had seemed to think that it was a good idea, too. So I took the money and started thinking about my next chapter. What did I want to do with the second half of my life?

I hadn't known at the time that Joe was asking himself the very same question. He arrived at his answer before I did. About a week after I'd accepted the offer from the *Trib*, Joe waltzed in from work and announced, without the slightest bit of warning, that he really wasn't in love with me anymore. We had nothing in common aside from a grown daughter. He wanted a divorce. And with that simple, matter-of-fact statement, my world had come crashing down.

Or, at least, that's how it had felt at the time. Over the past nine months since I packed up my things and came back to Thistlewood, I'd come to realize that maybe Joe had a point. I didn't miss *him* as much as I missed the *idea* of him, the idea of us. And eventually I didn't even miss that anymore.

I flipped the sign on the paper's front door to *CLOSED* and headed off toward Wren's house. There weren't many people milling about downtown, even during lunch hour, although I spotted a few walking in the direction of the diner. During summer, it would be very different. Traffic would congest Main Street like a bad cold. The locals would complain half-heartedly, because they all knew the money those crowds brought in during the summer was the only thing that kept groceries on the table for most residents during the winter.

Wren Lawson's funeral home, Memory Grove, is located on James Street, just off Main, behind one of the churches. It's a large, two-story Victorian on a deep lot that sits back from the road, with a big front garden where family and friends of the deceased can mingle. Wren's living quarters are upstairs, with the funeral home below and the mortuary itself in the basement. When she took over the business from the previous owner, Wren painted the exterior a beautiful robin's egg blue.

Just because it's a funeral home doesn't mean it has to look depressing, she'd said. This change from the somber gray that Memory Grove had been for generations had bothered some people in town almost as much as the fact that the new owner was African-American.

I walked through the front door and pulled it shut as quietly as possible. Stepping into Wren's house always felt like stepping into a chapel. A large staircase with angels on either side of the bottom posts stared back at me, their eyes watching my every move. Maybe even judging me a little. When I visit, I always tend to whisper until I'm upstairs. Which is a bit silly, I guess. As Wren often says, her overnight guests are very difficult to disturb.

"Ruth!" she called out from the top of the stairs.

"Hang your coat and come on up. I'm just finishing the chicken salad."

I crept into the foyer to hang my jacket on the coat rack. Then I headed upstairs, careful to stay toward the middle of the steps to avoid those judgy angels.

"Cassie isn't joining us?" Wren asked.

"No. She didn't know how long she'd be at the library. But she said to tell you hi, and that she'd see you later in the week."

Wren rolled her dark eyes. "Why on earth do you still think you can lie to me, Ruth Townsend? I've known you since you were fourteen years old, and I can spot your little white lies before the words ever make it to your lips."

I laughed. "It's not a lie."

Wren shook her head of auburn curls and said, "Cassie is spooked of my place. That doesn't hurt my feelings. Some people are just more sensitive about death than others."

"It's true," I admitted. "Cassie's had this thing with funerals since she was a teenager."

A thing was putting it mildly. Cassie had never said outright that she saw or even sensed ghosts. All I knew was that she refused to step foot into mortuaries or cemeteries, and most churches were off-limits, too. While I kind of understood her point about the funeral parlor itself, it was hard to see how anyone could be spooked here in Wren's cozy, colorful kitchen.

"I was kind of hoping I could get her to move past

it, now that I'm back in Thistlewood," I added. "Because you know she loves you to pieces."

"The feeling is mutual, but I'm happy to visit with her at your place until she gets over it. *If* she gets over it. You said yourself that Cassie senses things. A smart girl knows her limits."

"Thought you didn't believe in ghosts?"

"I never said that. What I said is I've never *seen* one. At my house, or anywhere else. Doesn't mean they don't exist. Doesn't mean other people don't see them. Given my line of work, I consider not seeing them a blessing. Could you imagine knowing a spirit was watching over your shoulder as you embalmed its body?"

Wren's dark brown eyes sparkled teasingly. She knew I couldn't even begin to imagine getting a body ready for burial, with or without a ghostly observer. Viewings, preparing bodies, dealing with grieving families…just thinking about the entire process made me shudder.

"Anyway," Wren said, "if I didn't believe in ghosts just a little, why would I have painted this place haint blue?"

"What on earth is *haint blue*?" I asked.

Wren laughed. "Ask Cassie. She knows. Do you want coffee before or after we eat?"

"Both, of course. And also *while* we eat."

Wren and I became friends in high school when her family first moved to Thistlewood. We'd stayed in touch easily while I worked in Nashville. Our friendship had always been the kind where we could go months without speaking and then pick back up as if no time had passed at all. She was always great about checking in on my parents when they were alive, and I'm not sure what I would have done without her during my divorce. Wren had made my transition back to Thistlewood as painless as possible, which was saying something, given the circumstances.

But I'll admit that her choice of career is puzzling. Why would someone with Wren's brains and beauty decide to become a mortician? Her military service had something to do with the decision. When she enlisted after high school, the recruiter had promised her a medical field. Her goal was to complete a single tour and have money for college, so she could become a physician's assistant or maybe go to medical school. As is so often the case, however, what the recruiter promised and what he delivered were entirely different things. Wren was trained as a mortuary affairs specialist. To her surprise, she'd actually liked the work, and she'd liked the military, especially since it gave her the opportunity to travel.

For me, the bigger question had always been why she chose to come back to Thistlewood to practice after her military retirement. The town is far from diverse, and as one of only a few black students, high school here hadn't exactly been easy for her. From what she'd told me, her brother had been baffled by that decision as well. They're still close, but she has to go to him—he won't even visit her here.

I'd asked her these questions when she told me her

plans. I knew that part of her reason for moving back was so she'd be around to help care for her grandmother during the last few years of her life. But Wren had also said that the job put her in a position to bring comfort to people. Maybe being there, offering kind words and helpful advice in their time of need, would bridge the divide a bit. Maybe she could help create some positive change.

Her first few years back in Thistlewood had been rough. She'd apprenticed with the former owner for a while, then bought him out when he retired. Most of the families in town had used Memory Grove for generations, and many of them continued to do so after Wren took over. Others weren't at all pleased that the previous owner had apprenticed a black woman, and they opted to take their business to a funeral home in Pigeon Forge instead. Not that they'd admit that was the reason why, of course. They'd just shake their heads and say that they couldn't imagine having a funeral in a place that was painted bright blue. *Haint blue*, apparently.

Over time, though, most of the residents had come to accept Wren's role in Thistlewood. So maybe she was right. Maybe she *was* making things better.

I opened the cupboard where she keeps her coffee mugs and poured both of us a cup. "So…what did you want to give me?"

"Ooh. You are a *greedy* girl today, aren't you?"

I grinned. "What can I say? I like presents. It's the only thing that makes birthdays tolerable at our advanced age. Well, presents and cake. And margaritas."

"It's just something I found at a thrift store." Wren heaped a few spoonfuls of chicken salad onto the pile of lettuce in the center of each plate. "A *little* something. My ship hasn't come in yet."

"You have a ship? I'd be happy with a rowboat."

Wren put the plates on the table, along with a basket of rolls. "I think Ed Shelton has a rowboat."

"So?"

She threw up her hands. "So. Maybe he'll take you out sometime."

I laughed and took a bite of the salad. "Maybe. We're not twenty-five anymore. Or forty, for that matter."

"Any big stories this week?" she asked.

"Bake sale down at the community center to raise funds for that gazebo they want to put in the park. Pretty hot ticket."

"I'm sure that will have copies flying off the shelves."

"Know of anything else? Maybe a planned jewel heist?"

Wren shook her head. "I wish I did. There aren't even any new obituaries to send you this week. It's like everyone in Thistlewood just decided not to die."

I laughed. "Good for them, I guess. Bad for business, though."

"It is what it is."

Wren's table sits in a little nook overlooking the front

garden below. We chatted about everything and nothing, and when we finished our lunch, she said, "Wait here, I'll be right back. You're going to love it!"

She returned a few seconds later with something hidden behind her back. When she reached the table, she presented it with a flourish—a brown cap like the ones newsboys used to wear when they hawked papers on city sidewalks. The fabric was warm and rough against my palm, instantly conjuring up images of busy streets, bells ringing, and young voices yelling, *Extra! Extra! Read all about it!*

I did love it. While I didn't know if I would ever *wear* it, I loved it just the same. Cassie would certainly get a kick out of it.

"Put it on," Wren said. She didn't wait for me, but instead grabbed the hat from my hand and placed it atop my head. And although it had looked a bit small, it was actually a perfect fit.

I stepped back and turned around in a full circle to model it for her. "How do I look?"

"Like a professional," she said, her dark eyes shining. "I'm so proud of you. You've been hit with a lot in the past year, and you've faced all of it with such strength."

"Well, I couldn't have done it without—"

My words were cut short by a shrill scream from outside. I followed Wren's gaze to the window. The door to Edith Morton's house next door was wide open. A small woman with fiery red hair spilled out onto the lawn. She was about my age, or maybe a bit older, but I don't think she went to school here. I knew her face but couldn't place her name.

She turned and saw us at Wren's window. By the time we made it downstairs and opened the door, she was standing on the walkway to Memory Grove. Her face was ashen as she clutched her chest.

"Call the police," she yelled, even though she was only a few feet away and we could have heard a whisper.

Wren took a step forward, catching the woman as she stumbled and nearly fell into the bushes lining the front porch.

"What's wrong?" Wren asked.

"She's dead," the red-haired woman wheezed. "Call the sheriff. Call an ambulance. Call *somebody*. Edith Morton is dead."

☆ Chapter Three ☆

THE RED-HAIRED WOMAN'S name hit me as I stood over Edith Morton's body. Her name was Elaine Huckabee. And she was right. Edith was most certainly dead.

Edith's body was the first thing I'd seen when I stepped into the foyer, where she was crumpled like a pile of forgotten laundry at the bottom of the staircase. As I drew nearer, it had become clear that her neck was twisted at an odd angle. I wasn't squeamish about crime scenes and dead bodies, having seen plenty of them while working at the *News-Journal*. Something about the woman's expression chilled me, though. Her eyes were wide, staring straight at me, with her mouth partially open as if gasping in surprise.

I looked past the body to the long wooden staircase, which had a carpeted runner going up the middle. Something was on the landing, and even though I knew I really shouldn't, I stepped over the body and went up to investigate. The steps creaked beneath my shoes, doing everything in their power to alert the authorities to the fact that I was intruding on a crime scene. Or rather, a *possible* crime scene. The most plausible explanation was that Edith, who was in her eighties, had simply stumbled and fallen to her death. But something about the look of utter surprise on her face made it hard to accept that explanation. I thought there was a very good chance that she'd been pushed. For that matter, the killer might still be in the house.

The last notion sent a surge of adrenaline through my veins, even though it seemed unlikely. Based on my previous experience, Edith had been dead for several hours, if not longer. Plus, Elaine Huckabee's shriek would have chased away even the most dedicated of serial killers.

When I reached the landing, I knelt down to inspect the shattered coffee cup at the edge of the stair runner. There were traces of a light-brown liquid among the shards of china. Not dark enough to be coffee. It might be tea, but if so, I believe Edith had added a little some-thing to her cuppa—whiskey, judging from the scent.

I startled at the sound of approaching sirens. They were very unnecessary at this point, since Edith was beyond help, but Wren wouldn't have known that when she called 911. Hurrying back down the stairs, I stepped over Edith's body and let myself out the front door.

A police car screeched to a halt, half in Edith's driveway and half in her front yard. It wasn't just any cruiser. The word *Sheriff* was stenciled across the side in blocky green letters. I rolled my eyes, wishing it had been the deputy. Steve Blevins is a jerk.

This assessment is based partly on my own high school experiences with him, back when he had a luxurious head of feathered blond hair, drove a cherry-red Camaro, and thought he was God's most gracious gift to the girls at Thistlewood High. His rock-star tresses were long gone, and you never saw the man without a hat these days—either the cowboy style he wears on duty or a baseball cap if he's not in uniform. This led me to suspect that his hair had given up trying to survive on a skull that thick. I'd bumped into Blevins a few times since returning to Thistlewood. The man's personality hadn't improved with age, and there was definitely no love lost between him and Ed. The fact that Steve's son, Derrick, was the one who smacked into Ed like he was a roadside pinata had only complicated an animosity between the two men that spanned several decades.

So, I avoided Blevins whenever possible. But like it or not, I was going to have to deal with him now. I decided not to mention my trip upstairs. If the information came to light, so be it, but I certainly wasn't going to volunteer anything.

"Ms. Townsend." Steve nodded to me solemnly as he approached Edith's door. I was pretty sure I detected a note of sarcasm, but it's rare for him to say anything without a verbal sneer.

"Sheriff," I responded casually, as if there wasn't a dead body lying only a few feet behind me.

"You were inside?"

He saw me coming out, so unless the door was a portal to an alternate dimension, he knew full well that I had been inside.

"Yes." I nodded toward Elaine, who was clinging to Wren like a piece of fruit that refused to give up the vine. "You'll need to talk to her. She found the body."

Sheriff Blevins gave Elaine the briefest of glances. "Thanks," he said wryly, "but I reckon I still know how to do my job."

That's one of at least a dozen reasons I've never liked Blevins. His attitude sucks.

"I'm going in," he announced dramatically.

"Okay. If you expect me to cover you, though, I'm afraid I'm not armed today."

He gave me a snide, half-second smile. "Still hilarious after all these years, Townsend. Guess your ex didn't appreciate your biting wit?"

Blevins disappeared inside, clearly pleased with himself for striking a low blow. Fifteen seconds later, he was back.

"She's dead."

"Really?" I stopped myself from rolling my eyes and calling him Captain Obvious.

"Did you take pictures?" he asked as his gray eyes scanned my hands, pockets, and finally came to rest on my head. It was at that moment that I realized I still had the brown newsboy cap on. Great.

"Of course not," I said. "That would be ghoulish. Edith deserves her privacy."

Blevins didn't seem too concerned about that, however—he'd left the door wide open, and Edith's body was clearly visible. I didn't like seeing her that way. True, I'd barely known her, but still…she was a person with a right to basic dignity. Still, I found myself wishing I'd brought my phone so that I could have gotten a shot of the shattered cup at the top of the landing.

"Are you certain?" Blevins asked. "No shots of the body for your little paper?"

"Yes, I'm certain. I was only inside for a minute." That was still far longer than Blevins was inside, but I decided it might be best not to mention that.

He pinched the bridge of his nose and sighed. "You're a reporter, Ms. *Townsend*. I was just making sure."

And that was the second reason I didn't like the man—the way he said my last name. I hadn't imagined it that time. He'd said the name *Townsend* like it was something foul he might find on the bottom of his shoe.

"No, I did not take pictures." I fully enunciated each word, speaking slowly and carefully to be sure that they penetrated. "And since it looks like you have work to do, I'll leave you to it. You know where I am if you have any questions. Should I have Elaine stay at Wren's until you get around to questioning the person who actually *found* the body?"

Blevins nodded but didn't say anything. He was already on his cell phone and walking back into the house.

You'll never be half the man Ed is, I thought as I picked my way back over to Wren's yard, high-stepping a pile of broken branches that the county hadn't bothered to pick up yet.

"You need to stick around for a bit," I told Elaine. "The sheriff wants to talk to you when he's done over at Edith's place."

Her face paled, which was saying something since she was already white as a ghost. "Me? Why me? I didn't do anything."

"You're the one who found the body," I pointed out.

She gripped Wren's arm hard enough that I thought she was going to break it. "Did you hear that? They think I killed her."

That seemed like an odd thing to say. True, I'd been thinking that she *might* have been killed, but again, the simplest explanation was that Edith tripped and fell down the stairs. It's a fairly commonplace accident for someone her age.

And, personally, I'd be a lot more certain if not for the teacup. I wasn't sure why it stood out to me at first, but then it hit me. If you're holding a cup and you trip, the liquid goes flying out. But this spill seemed very contained. It looked more like she dropped it. In fact, if the edge of the teacup hadn't landed on the section without carpet, it probably wouldn't even have shattered at all.

Gently, I began to pry Elaine's bone-white fingers from Wren's wrist. "No need to worry. It looks like an accident. Blevins just needs to get your statement."

"But what do I tell him?"

I shrugged. "How about the truth?"

Wren massaged her freed arm. "Maybe we should go inside and have some tea," she said, looking pointedly at me. "I'm sure *all* of us could use it."

I got the unspoken message loud and clear. *Please don't leave me alone with the crazy lady.*

She didn't need to beg. I would eventually need to interview Elaine for the paper anyway, and she might be more forthcoming before Blevins gave her the standard warnings about speaking to the press. Although he might not even do that given the likelihood that it was an accident.

"That's a good idea," I said. "Come on, Elaine. Let's go upstairs. I think you need to sit down for a bit. Catch your breath."

I'd worked on the editorial staff for the past eight years at the *Trib*, so it had been a while since I'd actually been out on a beat, interviewing witnesses and so forth. The shock was still new to Elaine, and I felt a little bad questioning her so soon. But interviews are an integral part of the job, and I was sure that I'd get clearer, more honest answers from her now over a cup of chamomile than I'd get if I tracked her down at home or work tomorrow. Even when people have nothing to hide, they often push traumatic events down into the recesses of their memory after a day or two.

Wren's kitchen was also comforting. Homey. If you could get past the fact that a funeral home lay just beneath the kitchen floor, that is.

By the time tea was served, Elaine was visibly more relaxed. Her shoulders were no longer hunched, and the frown lines on her forehead had softened. Her hands still trembled slightly when she picked up the porcelain cup, but all in all, it was a dramatic improvement.

Wren sat down next to her. "Do you want to talk about it?"

Elaine shook her head, but then after a moment of staring into her tea, she began talking anyway.

"I can't believe she's dead. When I got there, I rang the bell. Knocked on the door. And then I banged on it. She didn't answer, so I tried the knob and it just opened up." Elaine stopped and fearfully looked over at Wren. "Do you think I'll get into trouble for that? You know, just waltzing right in like I owned the place?"

Wren shook her head. "I don't think so, sweetie. I'm sure the police will be glad you did. And I know Clarence won't mind."

Clarence Morton was Edith's son. Her only child. He was my age but still lived with her.

Elaine's eyes shot back and forth between the two of us. "Clarence?"

"Yes. He'll be glad you found her," Wren said. "Especially since he's out of town this week."

I doubt Elaine caught Wren's tone. It wasn't something that would be obvious to anyone who didn't know her well, but Wren was leading Elaine somewhere. And something *did* seem off about Elaine's reaction to Clarence's name. It put her on edge again, although I guess that could simply be nervousness over having to talk to Clarence about his mom's death when he returned.

"Oh. He's out of town?" Elaine asked.

Wren nodded. "I saw him yesterday as he was loading up the car."

"Do you know where he went?" I asked.

"Probably heading up to the mountains for a few days. He does that sometimes. He has a cabin up there." Wren took a deep breath. "I think he needs a break every now and then. He's never said anything specific, but I got the impression that Edith wasn't all that easy to live with."

I took a sip of my tea. "What makes you say that?"

Wren started to say something, then glanced at Elaine and seemed to think better of it. "Just a...feeling," she finally said with a look in my direction that clearly said, *I'll tell you later.*

"That's actually why I stopped by," Elaine said, perking up a bit. "With Clarence out of town and all. I just wanted to check on Edith. Since she was all alone."

The sparkle from Wren's eyes disappeared as one eyebrow arched slowly upward. "Really? That was nice of you."

Elaine stood and thanked Wren for the tea that she had hardly touched. "I need to go talk to Sheriff Blevins. And then I'm going home. It's been a rough day."

Wren nodded. "Of course. Anytime. I'll show you out."

But Elaine slipped through the kitchen door without waiting on Wren. She seemed to be in a hurry.

I sighed and sat back in my chair as her footsteps echoed down the stairs. "Okay, so spill. Why do you think Edith was hard to live with?"

"A bunch of things, really. Clarence has been wanting to sell the house and move out of town for years. Said he'd be happy to take Edith with him or find her an assisted-living place where she could socialize more. But she was adamant about keeping the house. Clarence must have pressed the point, though, because just last week there was a realtor sign in the yard. I watched Edith march down the sidewalk, yank it up, and stuff it in the trash can. She was yelling at him that she was changing her will, that he wouldn't be able to sell the house even after she was gone."

"But why?"

"No clue. Old people get set in their ways sometimes. It's not a place that's been in her family for generations or anything like that. Her ex-husband bought it when they moved here back in the 1950s. That was a few years before he left town."

I stared out the window, where Elaine was pacing the sidewalk, waiting for Blevins to get off the phone. "Did Elaine seem a little on edge to you when you mentioned Clarence's name? I know she just found Edith dead, but that was odd. Plus, a minute ago she seemed surprised that Clarence was out of town, and then suddenly that's the reason she was at Edith's in the first place."

Wren grinned. "Okay, that was kind of mean of me. I set that trap on purpose. Elaine and Clarence have been sneaking around forever. The whole town knows it. I'm guessing it's why she ended up divorced about two years back. And there's only one reason they're not together."

"Why's that?"

"Because Edith said she'd cut Clarence off without a dime if he married her. That's why Elaine hated Edith Morton," Wren said. "And Edith hated her right back."

☆ Chapter Four ☆

THE *THISTLEWOOD STAR'S* front office is an unassuming single room attached to a large warehouse-like building behind it. Back in the day, Mr. Dealey and I spent most of our time back there in the press room, as we called it, setting the type, scanning the proofs. Then, each Tuesday evening, we'd print off a few hundred copies to deliver the next morning.

These days, however, I do most of my work on my laptop here in the front room and rarely venture into the back. Stella is missing a few parts, one of which arrived in the mail today. There's also a linotype machine that Mr. Dealey never got around to giving a name, to the best of my knowledge. I'm thinking I'll stick with the Tennessee Williams theme and call it *Blanche*.

Cassie might have been overstating things to say that I'm not a fan of change, but it was definitely true that I was more than a bit nostalgic for the old days.

When I'd first started working at the *Star*, Jim Dealey would sit at the table in the back room with several cases of type sorts, which is what they call the individual metal letters, arrayed in front of him. He'd compose the paper, sliding each letter, spacer, and punctuation mark onto a metal composing stick. When one line of type was arranged, he'd move on to the next, sometimes working from written notes, and sometimes setting the type on the fly as he wrote the story. I always found that kind of amazing. Like most people who have grown accustomed to computers with backspace and delete buttons, I'm used to ripping out words or even entire sentences. Mr. Dealey rarely changed anything.

At first, my job had been to put the metal sorts back into the little square boxes inside the type cases for each font. The upper case was always reserved for capital letters, which was where we got the terms *uppercase* and *lowercase* letters. At the end of the day, my fingertips and nails would be an inky black from handling the sorts. I quickly learned to paint my nails a dark shade to cover the ink that just wouldn't yield to soap and water. After a few months, Mr. Dealey began teaching me to set the type on the composing stick, one glyph at a time, backward and upside down.

By my junior year, I was writing stories as well, although I was never confident enough to compose the type on the fly. That same year, he bought the linotype from a weekly paper over near Nashville that closed down. I thought the machine was the most fabulous invention ever after manually setting the type for several years. It cut our work almost in half. That was probably the only reason Mr. Dealey was able to keep the paper going after his wife died and I went off to college.

He was happy to let me write up pretty much any story I wanted by the time I graduated, but he always wrote the obituaries himself. One of his quirks was his belief that everyone's obituary should be special. It was the person's final bow, their last time in the spotlight, and he wanted that paragraph, no matter how brief, to stand out from all the others that came before. He was determined that their last mention in the *Thistlewood Star* wouldn't blend in with the rest of the paper. Times New Roman simply wouldn't do. "Every obituary should have an individual face," he'd said.

That's why the back room is filled with type cases. There are hundreds of them stacked along the walls. Courier, Goudy, Bembo, Baskerville, Copperplate Gothic, Century Schoolbook, News Gothic, Gill Sans, Palatino, Mistral, Cooper Black. The font inventory list goes on for several pages, most with italic and bold variants. A lot of them also have a name and a date penciled in the margin. *Bill Peavy 10/3/82* is jotted next to the entry for Courier Italic. *Anna Bellamy 12/12/95* is next to Goudy. Each time someone from Thistlewood died, Jim Dealey would choose a new font for the obituary, never using the same typeface twice.

It was usually easy for me to tell how much Mr. Dealey liked someone from the font he chose for their obituary. If your entry was printed in an ugly font, or one barely distinguishable from the classified ads, he probably thought the world wouldn't miss you much.

When Mr. Dealey died, the paper closed. He had a part-time assistant, but no one to put out that last issue, and I didn't find out about his death until a few days later. His obituary had already been printed in the Maryville paper, in the same font as all of the others. That seemed wrong to me, so I called in a few favors and a separate notice ran two days later in *The Nashville News-Journal*, my old employer. It was set in the font *Joanna*, which had been the name of Dealey's wife. When she'd died during my senior year in high school, he'd composed her obituary in *Joanna Bold*, with tears streaming down his cheeks. And while every obituary should have an individual face, I thought that Mr. Dealey would appreciate me keeping the two of them in the same font family.

I hadn't been sure the typeface collection would still be there when I bought the paper. Metal type sets are occasionally sold to collectors on eBay, and I thought Mr. Dealey's son, who moved to Atlanta years ago, might have decided to sell them off. But the cases were still there when I purchased the building, and not just the ones I remembered. Mr. Dealey had added to the collection over the years, including a number of modern fonts that he must have special ordered because they were invented long after most newspapers abandoned ancient presses like ours.

"Well, Stella," I said aloud as I entered the press

room, "I guess we need to find a font for Edith Morton."

Stella didn't answer back, of course, but I felt her looking on approvingly as I thumbed through the font list. This was the first step to getting the *Star* back on track. I might have to enter the font on the computer for now, but eventually we'd get the press repaired, and I'd be in here setting the type on Blanche, just like the old days, and cranking out the assembled pages on Stella.

Edith's death was the first since the paper was reopened. I scanned through the inventory, looking for something that Mr. Dealey hadn't used. Since I didn't know Edith well, or really at all, I wanted to keep things fairly simple. Helvetica had been used for an obituary back in the 1980s, but there was no one assigned to Helvetica Bold. I thought it would do nicely.

Once I wrote Edith's name and the date next to the font, I went back to my desk in the front office. Four desks had been left behind when the paper closed down, although I didn't think there had ever been more than three people working here at any given time. I took the desk at the back, which had been mine before I left for college.

Every day, as I sat behind the other three desks working on my aging Mac notebook, I couldn't help but think how sad the office looked. Exposed brick, which once upon a time might have been fashionable by Thistlewood standards, now looked cold and dull. The large plate-glass windows that faced Main Street needed a good washing. There were a million little things, and some quite big things, that I needed to do.

But first I needed to get the story of Edith's death written down to be sure I didn't forget any details. Eventually I'd have to talk to Blevins again to verify cause of death, and I'd need to contact her son, Clarence, about the obituary, but first things first.

I had barely settled myself behind the desk when the little bell above the door announced Ed Shelton's arrival. He moved slowly toward the back of the building, favoring the right hip that had been shattered in the accident. It was a blue-eyed miracle that he survived at all, much less managed to walk again.

"Heard you were at Edith Morton's this morning," he said by way of greeting.

"Bad news travels fast, huh?"

"In a town this small? You bet."

Ed pulled a wooden chair up to my desk and collapsed into it, giving a little sigh of relief as his weight transferred off his bad hip.

"Poor Clarence." Ed's voice had a deep, almost rumbly quality that I'd liked from the moment we met. "His mom was about all he had. Well, aside from…"

"Elaine?" I asked.

He chuckled. "Well, look at you. Diving right into the gossip pool."

"Wren has her finger on the pulse of the town." I grinned, enjoying my little joke.

"Hey, Thistlewood isn't dead yet," he said. "You

know, you'd probably sell a lot more papers if you added a gossip column."

Sadly, Ed was right, but I wasn't inclined to toss my journalistic standards into the rubbish heap so soon.

"Getting back to Clarence," I said. "I know he took care of his mom, but...did he have a job?"

"Not since he moved back. He lived in Chattanooga for a while. Not sure what he did there."

"Do you know anything about their relationship? Not him and Elaine," I clarified. "With Edith."

"She was his mom. What more is there to know?"

"I'm not sure. Just something Wren said earlier. Something about Edith being hard to live with."

"Well, Wren would probably have a better idea than most, since they're neighbors. She and Clarence seemed to get along well enough to me. But you never know what people's lives are like behind closed doors. Good thing, too. Otherwise, we wouldn't need mystery writers, and I'd be spending my days watching *Judge Judy* or reruns of *The Rockford Files*."

"True."

After Ed retired, he'd started writing again. It was something he said he'd enjoyed when he was younger, but he'd never really had the time to pursue it during his years as a small-town deputy and even less once he became sheriff. He wrote police procedurals and mysteries, although he claimed there was some poetry and a teenaged attempt at a fantasy novel stashed away in a drawer. He'd published a few short stories, and then his first book was picked up by a small publisher,

Whodunit Press, last year. They modeled their novels after those old cold-case crime offerings of the 1970s. The covers were wonderfully nostalgic—scantily clad women holding firearms in various poses. Pulp fiction at its finest. In fact, it was at a signing for his first book, *Double Whammy*, at the local library that Ed and I first got to talking.

"Speaking of," I said. "How's the new book going?"

He frowned. "Anyone that tells you it gets easier is either lying or a complete moron."

"That bad?"

He settled back in his chair. "It'll work itself out. The people down in Atlanta seem to think so anyway. They're very happy with the second book. My editor says it's my best yet, although since it's my sophomore effort, I guess that's not saying too much."

I gave him a perturbed look. "So, when do *I* get to read it? I don't even know the title yet."

He smiled, crinkling up the corners of his eyes. That's another thing I like about Ed—his smiles always seem genuine. "It should be back from the copyedit in a week or so. I'll let you read it then, after most of my typos are cleaned up and it's presentable. I don't want to jinx anything."

Ed looked out the window, which reminded me again that it really needed to be cleaned. He had a pensive look on his face, like he always did when he was thinking something through. "So, you're thinking maybe it wasn't an accident?"

"I didn't actually *say* that."

"Why else would you be asking about her relationship with Clarence? Or saying that Wren thinks maybe she was hard to live with? What did you see at Edith's house that made you suspicious?"

I told him about the broken cup at the top of the stairs. "Probably just an overactive imagination, though."

"Maybe. But Edith was in good health for her age. I saw her down at the diner just last week talking to Patsy's mom. Let's just say I'm pretty sure she'd have beaten me in a footrace. Did you say anything to Blevins?"

"No," I said. "I kind of skipped the part about going up the stairs to check it out. He seemed a little annoyed that I went in the house at all. But I'm sure he'll find it on his own."

"I wouldn't count on it. Blevins couldn't find his butt with two free hands and a road map."

The bell above the door jingled again, and we both turned to look. It was Cassie. She gave us a sassy grin.

"Why, Mr. Shelton!" she said as she pulled up a chair from one of the other desks. "What brings you into the lonely offices of the *Thistlewood Star*?"

Ed smiled back at her. "Nothing lonely about this building. I quite like it, in fact."

She didn't back down. "Uh-huh."

"Actually," he said, "now that you mention it, I dropped by to ask your mother if she'd like to join me for dinner tonight."

"She'd love to," Cassie replied. "Wouldn't you, Mom?"

I glanced back and forth between the two of them. Why did I feel like they were ganging up on me?

"Sure," I said. "I'd love to."

Ed looked very proud of himself. "Well, it's settled, then. I'll pick you up around seven?" He framed it as a question, not as a demand, and that was another thing I liked about him.

Cassie wagged her eyebrows up and down. "He's picking you up," she echoed. "Around seven."

"Yes. I was sitting right here, so I actually heard that part. But thanks for translating."

Ed laughed and then added, "Would you like to join us, Cassie? You're more than welcome."

I felt something inside my heart warm. While I know you should never compare one man to another, it was hard not to with Ed. He was just about everything Joe wasn't.

"Thanks, Mr. Shelton," Cassie replied, "but I was planning to catch up on Netflix."

"Ed," he told her. "Call me Ed. And I'll see *you* at seven." He nodded toward me and then made his exit.

My daughter barely waited for the front door to close before rounding back on me. "Mom! What the heck?"

"Cassie, he's just a friend. Seriously."

"You know," she said, "it's not a big deal that you're dating. In fact, I totally approve."

"That's nice to know, I guess?"

"In fact, I think it's high time you got back in the saddle." She pushed the wheeled chair back over to its desk and headed for the door.

"Where are you off to?"

"I still haven't made it to the library," she said.

"Well, just to give a heads-up, some people may be a little upset. Thistlewood is a small town, and we've had a death this afternoon."

"Oh, no," she said, pausing at the front counter. "Is it someone you knew well?"

"Not really, but I was at Wren's when the body was found next door."

She shuddered. "A funeral home and a dead body. Very glad that I didn't take you up on that lunch offer."

"So am I. But you're going to laugh at what Wren gave me." I opened the desk drawer and put on the cap.

"That is seriously cool," she said.

I'd expected snort-laughs, so I gave her a skeptical look, bracing for the punch. But instead, she came over and inspected it.

"It suits you," she said, echoing Wren's assessment. "But you are not wearing it on your date tonight. And speaking of, I'm going to see if they have a copy of Ed Shelton's book while I'm at the library. It's not really my genre, but I'm interested now that he's, you know, *dating my mom.*"

"You're going to keep teasing me, aren't you?"

She nodded, grinning widely. "Oh yes."

"I have a copy of Ed's book at home."

Cassie reached the door. "Sure," she said, "but that's your special copy."

"Special?"

"Yep." She stepped out into the sunlight, which danced playfully across the purple highlights in her hair. "Signed by the author and everything. I bet it even says *Love, Ed.*"

☆ Chapter Five ☆

I WAS ACTUALLY GETTING ready for a *date*. The thought sent my mind racing around in circles. Joe hadn't really been the romantic type, so we never did the whole date-night thing that some married couples do. It had been well over a quarter century since I'd stood before a mirror prepping for a date.

At first, I tried telling myself that dinner with Ed wasn't anything out of the ordinary. We had shared meals before, even grabbed dinner at Pat's together on a few occasions when he stopped by close to closing time. I'd met him at his place when he hosted poker games. He'd never actually asked me *out*, though. Never picked me up. And something in his voice back at the paper had been different.

A date. At fifty.

Well, why not? I hadn't exactly planned on this, but Cassie was right. It was time to get back in the saddle. The end with Joe had come without warning. I was stunned to say the least. But I hadn't been *devastated*, and as I'd sat there at the kitchen table and listened to all his reasons why, that fact told me more than anything Joe was saying. After nearly thirty years, I should have been devastated, right? But I knew there was some truth in what he was saying. We had grown apart. And Joe had never been exactly easy to live with. I had put up with a lot, mostly for Cassie's sake.

Over the next few days, I had cried a few times, but there was only once when it hit me hard. I'd called Wren and told her I was going to talk to Joe that night, beg him to go to a counselor with me. She'd asked if I still loved him and I said *of course*, but as the words left my mouth, I'd realized they weren't entirely true. I just didn't want to be alone. And I didn't want Cassie feeling responsible for keeping me company. She had her own life. Wren convinced me that what I really needed was to get out of Nashville. Make a fresh start. By the end of the next day, I was packed. I'd taken what I could fit into my Jeep and left the rest for Joe to deal with.

There was light knock at my bedroom door, and then Cassie stepped in. She cocked her head to one side and met my eyes in the mirror. "Well, don't you look gorgeous?"

Gorgeous might be pushing it, but I did look pretty darn good. I was wearing dressy jeans I'd bought a few years back but never worn. Cassie had loaned me the sweater—a black, shimmery thing that clung to my curves more closely than anything in my own closet. Makeup, earrings, even a quick pass with the curling iron to give my unruly hair a hint of order. The woman in the mirror was still me, just with a bit more polish.

"I feel like I'm playing dress-up. But I do like the sweater."

"It's perfect. We need to take you shopping, though. Somewhere other than the Bargain Closet."

I grimaced, and we both laughed. It's no secret that I hate shopping with a purple passion.

She glanced down at the book in her hand, a slim volume with the title *Double Whammy* in a blocky font across the top and *Ed Shelton* in smaller letters across the bottom. "This ain't half bad," she said, thumbing absently through the pages. "Even if it's not the kind of book I usually go for."

I wasn't surprised, since her reading habits generally tended toward Dean Koontz. "Could use a few more government conspiracies and alien abductions, though?"

"An extraterrestrial subplot wouldn't hurt, but I'm definitely enjoying it. And I can also see similarities to Thistlewood in his story."

"The racist sheriff?"

Cassie wrinkled her nose. "I was thinking more the description of the diner. And the reporter he's crushing on."

"You do know that's a standard trope in mystery books, right?"

"Apparently it's a trope for a reason. Is the sheriff really racist?"

"Blevins? He was definitely a racist in high school.

Nothing else about his personality seems to have changed, so I doubt that did. He asked me out on multiple occasions, but he didn't like Wren. Told me I shouldn't hang out with her and her brother. Said people would get the wrong idea."

"Wow," Cassie said. "Did you know Ed in high school?"

I shook my head. "Not really. He'd been out of school for a while. He's quite a bit older than me."

The doorbell dinged, and Cronkite dashed past the open door. I've tried to tell him that this isn't appropriate behavior for a feline. He's supposed to be aloof and reserved. But in addition to—or possibly as a result of—his duties as guard cat, Cronkite considers himself the official greeter of the household.

"Aaaand he's here," Cassie said with a smile.

I blew out a sigh and headed for the door. Cassie stopped me by gently grabbing my arm. "Whoa. Where do you think you're going?"

"To answer the door."

"No, you aren't. I'll get it."

"Why?"

"Because that's the way these things are done. I'll get the door, let him in, and you wait a few minutes before coming down for the big reveal."

"Cassie. You can't be serious."

She bounced out into the hallway. "Oh, yes. I most certainly am."

☆☆☆

Ed picked a small restaurant called the Mountain View Grill. I'd never been there before, but the place definitely delivered on its name. Parked on a ridge with the entire back of the building in glass, the Mountain View had a breathtaking view of—you guessed it—mountains. The place would no doubt be hopping during the tourist season, but they had just reopened on the first of March, with limited hours until Memorial Day. I was glad to see they had a decent amount of traffic for off-season. As Ed and I entered, I counted maybe a dozen others.

With its wooden walls, exposed beams across the vaulted ceiling, and a crackling fire blazing off to my left, it felt like we'd stepped into someone's luxurious hunting lodge. There were no booths, only small tables topped with spotless white linens.

"What do you think?" Ed asked.

I smiled. "It's beautiful. Seriously, Ed."

"Can't hold a candle to you, though." He said the words so lightly that I almost wondered if I hadn't imagined them. I smiled at him, and then looked away to hide my blush. I would never have pegged Ed Shelton as suave, but I was beginning to think there were layers to his personality I hadn't discovered.

The hostess welcomed us as if we were family or long-lost friends that she hadn't seen in a month of Sundays. The stress of the day, of finding Edith's body, began to melt away as she led us to an open table near the back and promised to return shortly to take our order.

I took a moment to breathe in the scenery. Our seats overlooked a patio that ran the length of the building. It was unoccupied this evening—even the tables had been cleared away, most likely stored for the winter in a dark room, awaiting their days in the sun. Flood lights illuminated the corners of the patio, shining down on the dark, tangled mass of trees that dropped away into complete darkness below. It was a stunning view, beautiful, but also a bit scary.

Ed leaned across the table. "Happy birthday."

"It's the day after tomorrow," I said.

"I know. But I like to get a jump on things."

The waitress took our drink orders. We both asked for unsweetened tea, which seemed to surprise her.

When she left, Ed said, "She's going to think we're tourists," and we giggled like a couple of teenagers. He had a point. I wasn't sure if anyone else in Thistlewood even knew tea came unsweetened. At Pat's Diner, the tea has so much sugar that it doubles as dessert. Not that it keeps anyone from ordering dessert.

"I tried to call Blevins this afternoon," I told Ed. "After you and Cassie left. To verify cause of death."

"Well, what did he say?"

"Nothing. The phone rang and rang. I know he wasn't still at Edith's house, because I asked Wren."

"I'm sure he was just busy," Ed said with a sarcastic laugh. "We don't have too many accidents like that around here. Don't have too many people around here, period, so it's a case of basic math."

I took a sip of my tea. "There's something bothering me about that. The accident, I mean. Remember the broken coffee cup I mentioned just before Cassie came in?"

"Sure."

"Well, as an added point of interest, the carpet smelled like whiskey."

"So? You think she fell because she'd been drinking?"

"Maybe. Only…I'm not convinced that she *fell*, Ed. The cup looked like it dropped straight down. The spill was localized. Contained. Not spread all over heck and half of Georgia. If you fall with a drink in your hand, it goes everywhere."

I could practically see his thinking cap come on. "Maybe she had a heart attack and just dropped it?"

"It's possible. I guess we'll have to wait on the autopsy results."

"Except, there isn't going to be one."

"What?"

"There isn't going to be an autopsy. At least that's what Billy said when I ran into him on the way back home this afternoon."

Billy Thorpe had been a deputy when Ed was sheriff. He's still a deputy under Blevins, but let's just say he prefers his old boss to the new one. Billy's not the type to sit around and chatter about police business in the diner, but he keeps Ed informed.

"Why?" My voice must have risen, because the couple at the next table turned to look.

"Why," I repeated at a lower volume, "aren't they doing an autopsy?"

"Clarence," Ed said simply. "He said his mother wouldn't want one. Said she wouldn't want to be all cut up like that."

"And Blevins?"

"Well, he agrees. Edith Morton was eighty-five, after all. Everyone seems certain she fell."

"Not everyone," I said.

"Are y'all talking about that poor Morton woman?" the waitress asked. I hadn't even realized she was standing behind me. "It's so sad. The whole place has been talking about it tonight. Poor Clarence."

I tried to keep a sympathetic face, but the whole autopsy thing bothered me. If my mother had died in suspicious circumstances, I would have wanted to know.

The waitress nodded toward a tall young man sitting alone in the corner. He was dressed in blue jeans and a faded plaid shirt. I thought he looked familiar, but it took a moment for me to place him. It was Dean, the guy who delivered my mail. He was usually in a uniform, so I hadn't recognized him.

"Dean Jacobs is really torn up about it," she said, dropping her voice so that only Ed and I could hear her.

"Why is that?" Ed asked.

"Well, he's her mailman. He saw her every day. Said she always came to the door when she saw him coming." She took a deep breath and touched her heart. "He said he was there this morning. Knew something was wrong when she didn't come to greet him but thought maybe she was just under the weather."

"I want to talk to him," I told Ed as soon as the girl took our order and whisked off to the kitchen. "He may know something."

Ed reached out and touched my hand gently. "Wait until after dinner. We'll both talk to him."

I looked across the restaurant. Dean hadn't gotten his food yet either, so I thought it was pretty safe to wait. "Okay. But if he makes a dash for the door, I'm following him."

Ed laughed and shook his head. "I'll be right behind you."

☆ Chapter Six ☆

WREN SENT me a short text before we finished dinner. I squinted at the screen.

"Well, that seems fast," I said to Ed as I dropped my phone back into my purse. "Edith's visitation is tomorrow. Funeral on Friday." That meant I didn't have much time. I needed to get her obituary and information about services posted on the website by tomorrow, even though my next physical copy of the paper wouldn't be out until next week.

A thought occurred to me. "How much money do you think Edith was worth?"

He shrugged. "No clue. I do know she *had* money, though. Her house is one of the nicest in the county, and she used to drive that Mercedes around like she was some kind of movie star."

"But where did the money come from? Did she have a job or..."

"She did. Edith retired from that old factory out near the dump. Do you remember it?"

I nodded. "Vaguely. They made shirts, right?"

"Yes. She worked in the front office, but I think it was more to have something to do than because she really needed the income. Her husband used to own a couple of old hotels up near Pigeon Forge. Sold them right before he died in the eighties. And Edith got the money. They'd been divorced for a while. I guess he felt guilty about running off like he did."

"You'd think he'd have left the money to Clarence. I mean, he'd have been an adult by then."

Ed gave me a wry smile. "I think Clarence would probably agree with you on that point. But the will was written when Clarence was a kid, apparently, and his old man never bothered to change it. Edith gave Clarence anything he wanted. He may have had a job when he was living in Chattanooga, but he's been back here well over two decades, and I don't recall him working. So, Edith held the purse strings."

"Well, I guess he'll inherit now, won't he?"

"Yes, I would imagine so." He sighed and rubbed his face. "Dang it, Ruth. Now you've got me questioning things, and I don't like this feeling in my gut. It's rarely wrong."

I knew what he meant. I'd had the same feeling since this afternoon, and it wouldn't go away no matter how delicious dinner was or how charming Ed was. There was a dark cloud hanging over the Mountain View Grill. I could feel its weight as I choked down the last of my grilled chicken and asparagus, which I'm sure were both delicious, but I hardly tasted anything.

We were just finishing up when I noticed movement from Dean's table. He was signing the receipt.

"He's getting ready to leave," I told Ed.

"Here goes nothing, then."

We followed Dean to the front door. The waitress was watching us from the kitchen, part suspicious and part confused. We hadn't paid yet, and I could tell she was wondering whether the middle-aged couple, one of whom was the ex-sheriff, was about to dine and ditch. Ed motioned to her that we would be right back. She looked from us to the tall, broad-shouldered young man heading out the front door and nodded.

"Mr. Jacobs," I said as we stepped out into the cool night. "Could I speak with you for a moment?"

He startled. "Ms. Townsend?" The light in the parking lot was low, and I knew he couldn't see us clearly. "Ed? Is that you?"

"Hey, son," Ed said. His voice dropped down into a lower gear—his *cop voice*, as I had come to think of it. "Do you have a second?"

He took a few steps toward us. "Sure." Upon closer inspection, I couldn't help but notice how handsome he was. Nice guy, too, with a steady job. I wondered if he was single. Might be a good match for Cassie? I pushed the thought away. Her life was in Nashville. Although she seemed intent on playing matchmaker for me and Ed, I wasn't going to be *that* mom. Although it would kind of serve her right for teasing me.

"This is about Miss Edith, isn't it?" Dean asked, sticking his hands into the pockets of his black leather jacket. "What would you like to know, Ms. Townsend?"

"It's Ruth." I cleared my throat, wishing I had my notebook with me. "You were there this morning?"

He nodded. "A little after ten, as usual. I rang her doorbell several times."

"You didn't just put her stuff in the mailbox?"

Dean shook his head. "No, I usually bring it up to the door for her. Clarence is a little on the lazy side, if you ask me. He hardly ever checks the box, and Miss Edith doesn't get around so well anymore. Plus, I think she likes—liked—to have someone tell her good morning."

"Did you notice anything out of the ordinary today?"

He huffed, and then said, "It was totally out of the ordinary. Miss Edith answers the door right off the bat. Well, it sometimes takes a bit for her to get to the door, but she always shouts out that she's coming. She didn't this morning. I'd have thought she was at a doctor's appointment or something, but she mentioned yesterday that Clarence was out of town. I waited for several minutes. Even tried the doorknob."

I leaned forward. "You did?"

"Of course. I was worried about her. It was locked."

Locked? That struck me as odd. Elaine had said she just went right in. Even went so far as to wonder if she would be in trouble for doing so.

"You're *sure* the door was locked?" I glanced back at

Ed. In the darkness of the parking lot, I couldn't read his face.

"Yes. So, I put her stuff in the mailbox and went on with my route." Dean's eyes glistened with unshed tears in the darkness. "I should have called someone to check on her. They might have been able to save her. But I thought maybe she decided to sleep in for a change, so I just left."

I reached out and patted his shoulder. "No. I saw her body. I'm pretty sure she died instantly, and…probably hours before you arrived. There's nothing you could have done."

And I really *didn't* think there was anything he could have done. But my mind was whirling from his insistence that the door was locked.

"Ruth is right," Ed told him. "Don't even think about that, okay? Does no good at all."

"I know," Dean said. He wiped at his face, seeming embarrassed. "I need to get home. It's been a long day."

"Interesting," I said as the headlights on Dean's truck blinked to life. "Either Elaine is lying or someone else was at Edith's house this morning."

"Why do you say that?"

"She said the door was unlocked. Said she let herself right in."

Ed scratched his head. "I guess we need to tell Blevins, then."

I nodded. "But first we need to go inside and settle

this check. Our poor waitress is probably about to call the sheriff herself."

It was nearly ten by the time we made it back down the mountain and into Thistlewood. That's a late hour to call on someone, particularly the sheriff, but I knew I would have a better shot with a face-to-face meeting. He seemed to be ignoring my calls, which really left me no other choice.

The fact that Ed was with me complicated things a little, something he clearly recognized, considering that he offered to wait in the car. I had a sneaking suspicion that I wouldn't be there long, anyway. In fact, I'd be lucky if the good sheriff even answered the door.

Blevins lives in a medium-sized, two-story faux-log cabin on the edge of town, about a mile from Pat's Diner. There were lights on all over the bottom floor as we pulled in, and I caught glimpses of a flickering television behind gossamer curtains. Blevins was still up, as I had predicted—probably with a beer in one hand and a remote in the other. I just hoped he didn't answer the door in his boxers. Today had held enough horrors without that.

"Here goes nothing," I said to Ed. "Let's hope he doesn't shoot me before I make it up the driveway."

Ed shook his head. "Odds are he's already seen my truck. He knows it."

"That's part of the reason I'm afraid he might shoot," I said, and Ed responded with a laugh.

As soon as my feet hit the wooden boards of the

front porch, the light kicked on. I froze like a deer in the headlights. He *had* been watching.

"Well, well, well," Blevins said from the doorway. "To what do I owe the honor? And at this late hour?"

I was relieved to see he was completely dressed. In the exact same clothes I had seen him in earlier in the day, in fact, minus the hat. And my guess about the hat hiding a rapidly receding hairline was pretty much on point. To his credit, at least he hadn't adopted one of those awful comb-over styles.

"Can I come in?" I said. "It's kind of chilly. I need to talk to you about something."

Blevins glanced over my shoulder at Ed's idling truck. The heater thumped on and the sound seemed abnormally loud in the quiet of the night.

"Ed's not getting out?" Blevins raised his eyebrows.

"His hip gives him trouble in the cold."

While I half expected that little dig to get me bounced out on my ear, Blevins stepped out of the doorway. "Come on in," he said with a deep sigh that seemed to suggest this invitation was against his better judgment. "But be quiet. Jenny is asleep upstairs. Don't want to wake her."

I followed him into the cabin. He didn't need to worry about me waking his wife. Truth be told, I had always felt a little sorry for her.

The front door opened into a large living room and kitchen combo, a completely open space. There was a flat-screen TV above a darkened electric fireplace. The nightly news was flashing across the screen, muted, with the mouth of the news anchor moving a mile a minute.

Blevins sat in the recliner and motioned toward the vacant sofa across from him.

"So, what brings you and Ed out tonight?"

"It's about Edith Morton."

He nodded. "I figured as much. What about her?"

"Why no autopsy?"

"Not that it's any of your business, but Edith was eighty-five years old. She fell. That's all there is to it."

"But what if it isn't? I'm not convinced that she simply fell."

"Why?"

"Well, for one thing, there was the broken coffee cup on the landing upstairs."

He laughed softly, but there was nothing warm about it. "The coffee cup. So you went upstairs?"

"Yes," I admitted. "I noticed it, so I went up to investigate."

"And what do you think this coffee cup proves?"

I gave him my assessment of the situation: the cup, the spill, everything I had laid out for Ed back at the restaurant. Then I told him what Dean had said about the door being locked. When I finished, he didn't say anything. He just stared at me.

"Well," I nudged. "What do you think?"

Blevins stood up and stretched. "I think you're grasping at straws. I think you want a story. I think you're bored as the dickens in this tiny town after years as a big shot reporter in Nashville." He looked down at me. "Yeah, you *definitely* want a story, but this ain't it."

"How can you be so certain that Edith fell? Isn't it at least worth considering the possibility that something else might have happened?"

"Maybe Dean was wrong. Did you ever think about that?"

"No," I said, my voice rising. "Why aren't you taking this seriously? It's like this is some kind of joke to you. A woman died, Blevins."

"I know that, *Townsend*."

He glanced at the stairs along the wall. He cocked his head and listened, straining to hear any movement from upstairs. Once he was satisfied that all was quiet, he turned his attention back to me.

"I'm about to tell you something. Totally off the record, so I'd better not see hide nor hair of it in that little paper of yours."

"Okay."

He sat back down across from me. "I'm serious. Anything gets out from what I'm about to tell you and it's you I'll be arresting."

"Good grief," I said, "just tell me."

"I don't think Edith fell either."

A shiver traveled down my spine. "What?"

"I don't think she fell. She *jumped*."

Whatever I had expected Blevins to say, it wasn't this.

"Why would she do that? Why jump down a single

flight of stairs? Not even a full flight, actually, since she was on the landing."

I thought I saw a tiny flicker of doubt in his eyes, but then Blevins shook his head. "Edith Morton had a lot of problems."

"Her health?"

"In a sense," he said, scratching his scruffy beard. "Not her physical health, though. She'd been calling the station a lot, late at night, for the past few months. Said she was hearing music in the house. Getting strange phone calls, but never when Clarence was there. Called once to say someone had broken into the house. Sent a deputy out to check, and the only thing he could find was a broken window in the garage, but it was after that big storm last summer. Clarence told us she'd go off on rants, and that she'd taken to writing down dreams or… hallucinations, I guess, in her diary."

"What sort of hallucinations?"

"She claimed she was seeing ghosts."

☆ Chapter Seven ☆

WHEN I ARRIVED HOME, I learned that Clarence Morton had returned my call while I was out. Cassie had gathered the information for the obituary from him.

"Thank you, sweetie. That was a big help. Did he sound…okay?"

Cassie gave me a quizzical look. "His mother just died. I'm not sure what *okay* sounds like under the circumstances. To be honest, he sounded kind of numb to me."

I hesitated, not wanting to sound horrible, but also wishing I'd had the chance to talk to Clarence myself so that I could get a feel for things. I'm pretty sure that Steve Blevins thought telling me Edith was claiming to see ghosts would make me less inclined to believe that foul play had occurred, but it really didn't. If anything, I was more curious now than ever.

Part of the problem had been Blevins himself. He

wasn't friendly when I was at his place, by any means. There was still plenty of snark in his comments. But he'd given me information, and I really didn't get the sense that was his normal pattern when speaking with the press.

Since he'd referred to the *Star* as my "little paper," it could just be that he didn't consider me any sort of threat. He'd also made it very clear that I couldn't use the bit of information he'd given me, not that I would. Death is hard on a family, but suicide makes it so much worse.

So it wasn't really that he'd been nice, per se. It was more that he'd been nice for Steve Blevins. Ed agreed when I relayed the story to him, noting that Blevins had a policy of never giving any information to the press unless it was a formal announcement, and he avoided those except on the rare occasion when television cameras might roll in from Knoxville. Then he morphed into Mr. Congeniality, smiling for his close-up.

Cassie was my only hope of any additional information for the moment, so I decided to fish a bit more. "Did he mention Edith being...disturbed about anything recently?"

"Nope. Just what I typed up for the paper there. Her volunteer work, her surviving family—which is just him, apparently—and the funeral arrangements. Nothing about the cause of death, if that's what you're getting at."

"Well, I know the *proximate* cause of death. Her neck was broken from the fall. I'm just questioning the cause of that fall, and it doesn't seem that the sheriff is at all concerned about that. Just because someone is eighty-five years old doesn't mean you should automatically assume things. That's ageism."

Cassie smiled. "Funny how you're all of a sudden interested in ageism."

I stuck my tongue out at her. "I'm serious, Cassie. I went to see Blevins in order to tell him about two things that suggest something might be off about Edith's death. And all I got from him is the possibility—and you are sworn to secrecy about this—that Edith might have jumped. That she might have killed herself. I mean, seriously, who tries to commit suicide by throwing herself down a staircase? And not even the full flight of stairs, since she dropped her teacup on the landing. He's basing this solely on the fact that she had been calling the station lately with claims about seeing things."

"What sort of things?"

I hesitated again, because I wasn't sure that I wanted to get into this particular discussion with Cassie. "A ghost," I finally blurted out. "She kept calling, all distraught because some dark-haired boy was back, although he could never get her to give him any concrete information about what dark-haired boy and where or when he was from, except for the one time she admitted that he was dead. So yeah. A ghost."

Cassie shrugged. "Well, it's *possible*. I've known plenty of people who've seen them."

You mean you've seen them, I thought. But this probably

wasn't the best time to open that can of worms, so I stretched out on the bed next to her and watched the ceiling fan as it circled lazily above us.

"It could have been all in her mind, though. She was eighty-five. It's not uncommon for older people to hallucinate."

While I had never really talked to Edith, I'd seen her around town just like anyone else, and she'd always seemed pretty spry and savvy to me. Her obituary noted that she'd continued to volunteer even as an old lady. Dean hadn't mentioned anything about her being mentally unstable, and he'd spoken to her nearly every day. Maybe it was just a matter of not wanting to speak ill of the dead?

I pulled the covers up around my shoulders. Thinking back on the conversation with Blevins chilled me all over again. It had been a relief to get out of his house and crawl back into the warm confines of Ed's truck.

Cassie sighed. "Like I said, I believe it's *possible* that she saw something. But…there are usually *other* perfectly natural explanations for paranormal sightings. Someone could have been playing games with her. Making her believe she saw something that wasn't there. If she was on medication, they could have mixed them up or substituted them. There are lots of ways to mess with someone's head to push them over the edge."

"But with someone as old as Edith…I mean, there would be *easier* ways to kill her, don't you think? Old people die in their sleep all the time. I think they'd be even less likely to suspect foul play if she accidentally overdosed or simply stopped breathing than after finding her at the bottom of the stairs with her neck broken. Either way, though, Clarence would seem to be the most likely suspect. He lived with her."

"True," Cassie agreed. "And you did say he stands to inherit a lot of money. Maybe he got tired of waiting on her to die so he could collect?"

"Which is sad. Thank god I'll never have to worry about that. If you need what little money I have, just let me know, okay? We'll work something out."

Cassie laughed. "Is Sheriff Blevins friends with Clarence?"

"I don't know if they're *close*, but Ed says they're friends. And I did get the sense that the decision not to insist on an autopsy was more of a personal matter than anything professional. So I don't know if it's friendship, or maybe Blevins and Clarence are in on something together."

Cassie gave me a sly smile. "Ooh. A conspiracy."

Her saying the word made me realize that Blevins might be right. I'd been thinking just that morning that what the town needed was a good mystery if I wanted to sell papers. Maybe it was simply boredom convincing me to connect dots that really didn't make a picture.

Maybe.

But I really didn't think so.

"Well," I said, "either way, I have to get Edith's announcement in the paper. Or rather, on the website.

She'll get her *actual* obituary on Wednesday, in her own special font."

"You're going to continue the tradition?" Cassie asked.

I nodded. "I'm sure that the town doesn't really care one way or another. They probably think it's a silly custom. But it mattered to Mr. Dealey, and this way, the *Thistlewood Star* will continue to be his paper, even though he's gone."

Cassie snuggled up next to me, just like she used to when she was small. "You're such an old softy. That's one of the things I love most about you. An old softy... with a *boyfriend*."

☆ Chapter Eight ☆

THE MORNING of Edith's funeral was cloudy and cold without the promise of sun or warmth. It was also my birthday, which hadn't slipped Cassie's mind. She had been walking around all morning humming "Happy Birthday to You." But at least I hadn't come downstairs this morning to find balloons and streamers everywhere. I'd been a little worried that I might.

I found a black dress in the back of my closet. Circa 2005, but it still fit, so it would have to do. Cassie was right...I really needed to go shopping. It wasn't lack of money. I would never be in the market for designer labels, but I could afford a wardrobe makeover. I just hated the thought of it. Give me a few pairs of well-worn jeans, comfy sweaters, and a big warm jacket, and I am a happy woman.

I'd just pulled on a pair of ancient black heels when Cassie gave a light tap on the door and stepped inside.

"How do I look?" she asked.

We'd made a quick trip to the mall yesterday because Cassie hadn't packed for a funeral. Her black dress was a little tighter and shorter than mine, but still modest. She looked beautiful, and I felt that rush of pride that comes from watching your child grow into a strong, independent woman. I was quite certain there would be a few people in town who would take issue with her purple highlights, but people in small towns always need *something* to talk about. Life gets boring, otherwise. Might as well make it easy on them and dish up a teensy bit of scandal on a silver platter. That way they don't have to go snooping around for their gossip.

"You look stunning," I told her. "As always. And I really do appreciate you going. As long as you're *sure* you want to. Because you don't have to. You didn't even know Edith. I barely knew her."

I'd been completely surprised when Cassie offered to attend the service with me. It required her to actually step foot inside a room with a dead body, something that she'd done precisely once in her life, to the best of my knowledge. She'd had such a bad reaction when my parents died that I didn't press the point when her dad's mom died a few years later. There's no law dictating the way people grieve. While there were a few people who clearly didn't approve of a sixteen-year-old skipping her grandmother's services, I'd told her what they thought really didn't matter. Her father hadn't been too happy about it, but he'd seen how she reacted at my parents' funeral, and he was smart enough not to say too much to Cassie about staying home.

"I'll be okay," Cassie said, although I could see that she was a bit on edge. "I need to move past this. And I have to admit, I'm curious. If Edith was being haunted by some dark-haired boy, perhaps he'll be there today."

"And you think you'd actually *see* him?" I asked.

She gave me a grim smile. "Let's just say it wouldn't be the first time something like that has happened."

I hugged her tight. "Okay, sweetie. But I know this isn't easy for you. And I'm serious. If you need to make yourself scarce, I will understand *completely*."

Downstairs, the doorbell rang. It was probably Ed, who had offered to give us a ride to the service.

"I'll let your knight in shining Silverado in," Cassie said.

Cronkite rubbed against my leg and then darted after her, eager to help answer the door. But he stopped cold just beyond the threshold. In that spooky way that cats possess, his green eyes roamed over to the bedroom window and locked on it.

Ghosts.

I shuddered, shaking the word out of my head. "What is it, buddy?"

Stepping across the room, I pulled the curtain back, almost certain that a spectral face would jump out at me from the other side. But when I looked down into the yard, I smiled. It wasn't a ghost at all. Just Remy's furry black face poking through the underbrush. The bear must have seen the curtains rustle, because he was looking straight up at the window. It almost looked like he was smiling.

As I raised my hand to wave, a crazy thought struck me. Remy had come to tell me happy birthday. Somehow, he knew. I waved again and sent him a silent thank-you.

It was a profoundly silly thought. He probably wasn't even looking at this window. More likely it was a trick of the light, and he was just sitting there at the edge of the woods, wondering if I still had any of the berries and carrots I'd fed him when he was in my shed last year.

The bear didn't know it was my birthday.

But everyone is entitled to a few silly fantasies now and then.

☆☆☆

Death in a small town is a strange thing. Everyone pretends to know the deceased, to have been friends with them, even if they hadn't known them any better than I'd known Edith. The word always spreads quickly, especially when the death was sudden or accidental. I'm guessing half the county knew Edith was dead before my notice went up at the *Star Online*.

Edith's service was no different. Most of the town seemed to be there, along with a smattering of less-familiar faces who lived in the even smaller communities scattered around the county. Wren had said the visitation at the funeral home the night before hadn't been nearly as crowded, but then that's usually the case around here. Casual friends sometimes attend visitation, but it's mostly for family and close friends of the deceased.

The preacher Clarence asked to speak at the funeral wasn't from Thistlewood, so I suspected he was one of their distant relatives who traveled here from out of town. Most families have a cousin or an uncle who's a preacher of some sort, and they always seem determined to speak at the service, even if they haven't seen the deceased since a family reunion decades ago. This particular minister, whose name I didn't catch, spoke of Edith's life for only a few minutes and then launched into a full-on fire-and-brimstone sermon, clearly trying to preach poor Edith into heaven. After sitting through one of these funerals with my mother back when I was a teenager, she'd said I shouldn't bother with that at her funeral. If she hadn't made it into heaven by the time the service started, no amount of preaching was going to get her there. When the time came, I was glad she'd given me that bit of instruction. I was also glad that we didn't have any fire-and-brimstone types in the extended family, insisting on their moment in the spotlight.

Edith's mahogany casket shone brightly beneath the muted light. The church's stained-glass windows cast the colors of the prism across her body as a last tribute during Edith's final hour above ground. That sounds a little fanciful, I guess, especially after my earlier thoughts about the bear. But odd thoughts have always popped into my head during church, and even more so during funerals.

I knew Edith's son, Clarence, even less than I knew her. In fact, I'd have been hard-pressed to describe him, but the face clicked when I saw a man about Ed's age, or maybe a little older, following her casket down the long church aisle, out the door, and into the waiting hearse. Clarence Morton was short and overweight, although not exactly fat—sort of like a former football player who had given up exercise instead of beer. His eyes were dry but red and vacant, with dark circles underneath. He looked like he hadn't slept in days. And maybe he hadn't. It was a hard thing to lose a parent. I knew that from experience. But I had no idea how it felt to think your mother committed suicide. That had to make it so much harder.

The one absence that seemed notable was Elaine Huckabee. Even if she hadn't liked Edith, you'd think she'd have come to the service to support Clarence. I mean, if everyone in town knew they were an item, what reason did they have to hide it now? Unless there was a provision about that in the will, too? *My entire estate is bequeathed to my son, Clarence, as long as he doesn't sell the house, is never seen in public with Elaine Huckabee, and always remembers to wipe his feet on the front mat. Otherwise, he gets NOTHING.*

Compared to the funeral, Edith's graveside service was short and somber. This time, the speaker was Edith's own preacher, Reverend Walden. He said a few words about her years of service to the church and her community, casting a rather annoyed glance at the other preacher, who hadn't really bothered with those points.

Then he spoke a short prayer, and they lowered Edith's casket into the grave.

The crowd was sparse, too. Maybe people had already had their fill with the first service, or more likely the weather had driven them back home. There were barely two dozen of us gathered at the gravesite to pay our respects. Wren was there, but she was in her official capacity as funeral director now, so I just gave her a little wave and stuck close to Ed and Cassie.

It was cold, with the sun hiding behind big dark clouds. My dress wasn't nearly as warm as I'd have liked, and Cassie's apparently wasn't either. She was shivering, huddled between me and Ed as if we could shelter her from the biting Tennessee wind. Although in her case, I couldn't entirely discount the possibility that her shivering was only partially due to the wind chill. I doubt that anyone is ever really comfortable at a funeral, but Cassie had sat like a statue inside the church. Looking like she'd rather be almost anywhere else, her eyes kept scanning the room. When I'd asked if she wanted to skip the graveside service, she'd said no, and again, once we arrived at the cemetery, her eyes kept moving, slowly surveying the grounds as the minister spoke.

When the last shovelful of dirt had been turned over, Clarence stood in front of the freshly placed flowers and cleared his throat as everyone turned their eyes toward him. "I just want to thank you all for... uh...coming to Mom's service. It would've made her happy to know all of you cared enough to brave this cold day." He wiped at his eyes, even though I hadn't seen a hint of tears. "We'll be welcoming family and friends back at the house. Please stop by. There's more chicken and casserole there than one man could possibly eat."

He smiled, and there was a polite smattering of laughter among the crowd. I searched his face for something. Some telltale sign that my suspicions about him were unfounded. That he hadn't pushed Edith to her death on the promise of a windfall. Yes, he had been out of town, but in a cabin with no witnesses. That seemed awfully convenient to me.

And I guess the real problem was that there was this little tiny voice in my head that kept asking whether you could entirely blame him if he *had* pushed her. From the sound of it, his own mother had taken money that really should have been left to him by his father and used it to dictate his life. Here he was, at best only a few decades from the grave himself, and even now, he was at the funeral alone.

When the service ended, Cassie and I followed Ed back to his truck. She got into the backseat and I climbed up next to Ed, who quickly started the heat. My fingers were numb, and I began massaging them in front of the heater.

"Do you mind if we stop by Edith's house?" Cassie said from the backseat.

Ed shrugged. "Sure. I don't have anything pressing."

I'd never mentioned anything about her aversion to

funerals to Ed, so I didn't want to say anything openly. Instead, I turned and gave her a questioning look. *Are you sure?*

"I'm fine, Mom. I know you want to go, and I think you're right to be suspicious. Something feels off to me, and if there are any clues to be had about Edith's death, her house seems like the best place to start."

She was right. I definitely wanted to go. I'd just been worried about pushing her too far too soon.

"Okay, then," Ed said. "Let's go do some post-funeral sleuthing."

☆ Chapter Nine ☆

I STEPPED through the doorway of Edith's house, my eyes frozen on the exact spot at the bottom of the stairs where I'd seen her body. There was nothing there to suggest anything at all had happened in that section of the house, which shouldn't have surprised me, but somehow it did. I didn't really think that it would be marked off with tape like you see on the police shows, but it was just a square piece of hardwood flooring weathered over the years by countless footfalls, sunlight, and dust. It felt like there should be flowers, maybe, or one of those wooden crosses often seen on the side of roadways to mark the spot where someone died in a car accident.

The house was crowded. Even those who hadn't bothered to drive out to the gravesite had apparently still gotten the memo. Heads were bowed in quiet conversation, whispering, and soft laughter traveled through the air as if we were attending a cocktail party.

Suddenly I felt very much out of place. I didn't really know these people anymore. Maybe coming here had been a mistake.

Ed put a reassuring hand on my shoulder. "Are you okay?"

I nodded, and together we walked in. Cassie followed, her eyes again scanning the room, clearly searching for something or someone. She seemed uneasy too.

"Do all funerals end like this?" she asked. "With a…party?"

"For the most part, yes. There's been a reception of some sort at most of the funerals I've been to. Even when we lived in Nashville, they tended to invite family and friends back after the service. Although I think in a small town like this, more people might take them up on the offer. But keep in mind that almost everyone here also sent a casserole or a *pie*."

"Ah-ha," Cassie said. "That's where that second apple pie went. I thought you'd just gotten extra hungry in the middle of the night."

Ed laughed. "A whole pie? I doubt Ruth could manage more than a slice. Two at the most."

I smiled demurely. It was probably a good thing that he hadn't been around to witness my post-divorce consumption of Ben & Jerry's.

The kitchen and dining room had been turned into a potluck buffet. Dishes in aluminum pans and Tupperware containers were spread out on all available surfaces, along with plates of fried chicken, potato salad, cakes, and pies. Thistlewood had circled the wagons, as they say, and Clarence had been right. There was way more food than any one man could ever hope to eat.

Apparently our discussion in the hallway had whetted Ed's appetite for pie. He helped himself to a slice. Cassie and I settled for some coffee and went in search of an out-of-the-way corner to stand.

Clarence was in the parlor, where a long line of friends waited to speak to him. I thought about joining them but figured I'd hold off a few minutes. Maybe let it clear out a bit. I've never been good at talking to people in these types of situations. I'm always deathly afraid that I'll say something asinine, and if that happened, I'd prefer to have a smaller audience.

Ed was standing in the doorway chatting with Carl Smith, one of his poker buddies. He's much better at the socializing thing than I am, but then he'd have to be. I'm sure he's been to far more funerals, given the years that he spent as sheriff. Plus, the job requires an election every four years, so you have to learn how to engage in small talk. His main challenge seemed to be steering clear of Blevins, who was at the center of a small group of people across the room.

I turned to say something to Cassie and found that she'd wandered off. Maybe she decided to get some food after all. In search of something to do so that I didn't feel quite so awkward, I went over to the table that had been set up with pictures of Edith. A few were recognizable—Women's Club yearly photos, and one rather awkward picture of her with a little dog, who must have crossed the Rainbow Bridge before his owner. Others were from her youth. She'd been very pretty, tall and curvaceous, with dark hair that fell around her shoulders. Something about her smile in a few of those pictures seemed familiar, and I stared at one of them for a long time, trying to figure out where I'd seen it before. I didn't think it was simply that I'd seen an older version of that smile on the few occasions when I'd run into Edith Morton. Older Edith's smile was nothing like this. It was formal, reserved. It never looked like she was about to burst into laughter.

As I flipped through the album, I realized someone was watching me. I casually scanned the room from the corner of my eye to see who it might be, eventually arriving at an old man sitting across the room. There was something about his eyes that I didn't like. They weren't warm at all. In fact, they seemed slightly reptilian.

The old man didn't break the stare when I caught him, and I was determined not to be the first to look away. After a moment, he struggled to his feet, and using a shiny black walking stick, clacked his way over to where I stood.

"You're that newspaper chick, aren't you?"

I bristled but tried not to let it show. I'm generally hard to offend, but *chick* is one of the words that sets me off. It was all too easy to imagine this guy at the height of the disco era. Middle-aged, already balding, wearing a gold chain and a leisure suit, and totally convinced that he was hot stuff.

"Ruth Townsend." I offered my hand for him to shake. "And yes, I own the paper."

"Samuel Winters." He took my hand in his own. "Everyone calls me Sam. Nice to officially meet you. Just wish it were under different circumstances."

To my surprise, he didn't shake my hand. Instead he bent forward and delivered a papery dry kiss to the top. I'm sure he thought it was a courtly gesture, but I was instantly repulsed. It took everything I had not to jerk my hand back and slap him with it.

Instead, I simply pulled it away and said, "Nice to meet you, too."

"Did you know Edith well?" he asked, leaning forward on his walking stick.

"Not especially. Did *you* know her well?"

Sam smiled and took another step forward. My back was against the wall now, and I couldn't move away without bumping into either him or the walking stick.

"Yes," he replied. "You could say that. Edith worked for me for many years."

"At the garment factory?"

"Indeed. She was a godsend in that office. Best bookkeeper I ever had."

Sam glanced over at Clarence, still on the sofa accepting condolences. I could tell the old man was deep in thought about something. Maybe thinking about Edith manning the phones and balancing books

so long ago. Had they been in a relationship back in
the day?

"Edith came to me for a job when her husband left
her. He owned several hotels up near Pigeon Forge.
That town had just started to boom back then. He
moved up there when Clarence was barely out of
diapers. Took up with someone else, from what I
heard."

So Edith had gotten a job to help support her and
her son. While child support was a thing back then, I
suspected that it wasn't enforced nearly as strictly as it is
these days. From the little I had gathered about Edith
over the past few days, she seemed like a proud woman.
She might not even have sought money from Clarence's
father.

On the other hand, I kind of doubted that. She'd
apparently held on to his money really tight when she
finally got it.

"I gave the girl a job. Made sure she and the boy
were able to keep food on the table. Then she up and
quit."

"When her ex-husband died and left her money?" I
asked.

At first Winters didn't answer. He looked disturbed,
almost angry. "Obviously," the old man said finally.
"Otherwise she'd have stayed at the factory.
Otherwise…"

He looked around for a moment while I continued
to study his lined face. What had I said to trouble him?
Finally, his eyes settled on someone across the room.

"I need to talk to my grandson. Nicholas," he yelled, or at least tried to. It came out more as a hoarse whisper. "Nicholas."

A man in his late twenties turned toward us. He was rather short, and his black dress shirt was stretched tautly over a body that looked as if it had been chiseled from stone. He was talking to Cassie, and they seemed to be having a nice conversation. I envied her. She had definitely gotten the more pleasant of the two.

"Well, I see you've made a friend," Sam said as they approached.

"Actually, we'd already met," the young man said, smiling at Cassie. "I saw her at the diner earlier this week and I complimented her taste in books."

"Then you wasted a conversation, Jeffrey." The younger man opened his mouth like he was going to protest, but his grandfather kept going. "You should have complimented her lovely eyes. What's your name, sugar?"

Cassie started to speak, but I interrupted her. "This is my daughter, Cassandra Tate."

"Just Cassie," she said with an odd look at me. I never introduced her as Cassandra, but for some reason, I didn't want this old creep to know anything personal about her, even something as innocuous as her nickname.

"This house…it belonged to Edie…" Sam leaned on his stick again, looking confused. Fortunately, he didn't reach for Cassie's hand to kiss it like he had done with mine. If he had, I'd have been tempted to yank the stick out from under him. That would have been quite a scene for a funeral. No one would have soon forgotten it, and I doubt they'd be lining up to buy newspapers from the crazy woman who'd kicked the cane out from under an old guy who had to be at least ninety.

The grandson reached out to shake my hand. "Nick Winters. Very nice to meet you, Ms. Townsend."

"Ruth. It's a pleasure to meet you, too." I smiled a little more brightly than I might otherwise have, probably because I was feeling guilty about my intense dislike of his grandfather. It wasn't Nick's fault the old man was an obnoxious old coot, and it was clear that Sam Winters's mind was no longer firmly on track.

"Jeffrey, find your mother and tell her it's time to go."

Nick gave a half grin. "I'm not Uncle Jeffrey, Grandpa. I'm Nick."

"Of course you're Nick," Sam said angrily. "Whoever said you weren't?"

"Why don't I get you back to your chair?" Nick cajoled. "You've got a piece of cake over there you've barely touched."

"That ungrateful Mexican probably took it. He takes everything else, the dirty bean—"

"Grandpa! Cake!"

Nick walked the old man back over and then joined us again.

"I hope my grandfather hasn't been talking your ear off," he said, smiling apologetically. "And I'm sorry he backed you into the corner. He was quite the ladies' man back in the day, and he always seeks out a pretty face to chat with. But he's grown hard of hearing and doesn't want to admit it, so he gets right up in your face. And I'm afraid sometimes his mind wanders. He can tell some really wild stories when he gets going, and he has absolutely no filter."

"Oh, it wasn't a problem," I lied. "I hadn't even noticed. Are you about ready to leave, Cassie? I'll just speak with Clarence later. There are so many people here, and I'm sure he's feeling overwhelmed."

Cassie hesitated for a moment, and then said, "Sure. I just need to visit the restroom. It was nice seeing you again, Nick."

"I'll find Ed," I told her, anxious to get out of the room. "We'll meet you at the front door."

When I located Ed, he was talking with Clarence. I stepped in and told Clarence how sorry I was about his mother, and when the next person stepped forward, I whispered to Ed that we were ready to go.

"Me, too," he said. "Too many people. I'm starting to feel claustrophobic."

We went to the door and waited for Cassie. Ed introduced me to a couple who was leaving. He knew the woman from the local Kiwanis Club, and I realized I went to school with the guy, although I'd never have recognized him on the street, since he's nearly a hundred pounds lighter now. When he heard that I'd lived in Nashville, he said they had a daughter currently at Vanderbilt, which reminded me that my own daughter still wasn't back. I was about to go upstairs to check on her when I spotted her at the bottom of the stairs, talking to Nick Winters.

"What took so long?" I asked.

She gave me a look that clearly said *not now.* Then she continued toward the door, clutching her purse against her chest like a shield.

"Did you see something?" I whispered. "You're white as a sheet."

"Yes, you are," Ed said, with a concerned look. "Come on, let's get you out of here."

When we reached the truck, Ed unlocked the door and then went around to the driver's side.

"What's wrong?" I said softly. "Did Nick Winters say something to you?"

"No. I just...I think I found Edith's diary," she whispered, glancing nervously at Ed.

My mouth dropped wide open. I gave her one last perturbed look and then climbed into the Silverado.

We definitely were *not* having this conversation in front of Ed.

Chapter Ten

WHEN WE ARRIVED BACK at the house, I discovered that Cassie had somehow managed to bake a cake and buy me a tiara with *50 & Fabulous* in rhinestones. She invited Ed in, and they did the whole *Happy Birthday* routine, complete with slightly off-key singing and candles.

It was a sweet gesture, but I spent most of the time staring at Cassie's purse. It was the only place she could have hidden the diary, plus she hadn't let the darn thing out of her sight since we walked in the door.

Once we'd finished our cake, which Ed made room for despite the wedge of apple pie he'd eaten at Edith's house, he said that he needed to get back home and try to get a bit of writing done. I walked him out to the truck and thanked him for escorting us.

"You sure Cassie's okay?" he asked. "She seems kind of jittery."

I assured him that she just wasn't good with funerals. As soon as his truck was out of the drive, I hurried back into the house.

"You did *what?*"

"Okay, Mom, first of all...I'm going to need you to lower your voice."

"*You. Did. What?*" I hissed.

Cassie cringed as she pushed the small black leather notebook across the counter toward me. "I found Edith's diary," she repeated. "There are recent entries. Take it."

I stared at the book as if I was afraid to touch it. And I'll admit, there was a small part of me that *was*. The word *Journal* was embossed in the spine, with the current year written in marker just below.

"Oh, Cassie. Why?"

She went behind the counter, picked up Cronkite, and sat down at the kitchen table. The cat looked suspiciously between the two of us, probably sensing that he was being used as a feline shield.

"I'm not sure," Cassie said. "It was almost like I *had* to take it. The only reason I even went was because I... had this feeling. And when I realized what it was, something came over me."

"What? The urge to commit a crime? Where did you find it?"

The last question was the one I had dreaded asking. I hoped...really, *really* hoped that she hadn't been upstairs prowling through poor Edith Morton's personal things. Clarence had been busy, obviously, but there was still a chance that someone could have walked in on her.

"I *did* go to the bathroom," she said. "That part is true."

"Okay."

"And when I was coming out of the bathroom, my earring fell out. I swear. It was like fate."

"Fate." I looked at her skeptically. "Go on."

"The earring practically flung itself across the hall and into Edith's room."

"How did you know it was Edith's room?"

"It was full of old pictures and quilts, Mom. I can spot an old lady's bedroom. Also, it had that...smell. Like baby powder and mothballs. Anyway, I bent down to pick up the earring and there it was." She patted the diary. "Under the nightstand, wedged against the wall. It's recent. The last entry was a few days ago."

I finally picked the book up. Holding it away from my body as if it might bite at any moment, I carried the darn thing over to the table.

Cassie looked up at me. "Are you angry?"

I thought about that for a moment. Was I? "No," I decided. "I'm just surprised. A little scared, too. Blevins knows Edith kept a diary. He mentioned it when I was at his house. Said Clarence thought it might contain a note or some clue. So...they could be looking for this."

All of the color drained from Cassie's face, and I instantly regretted sharing that bit of information with her.

"Blevins was in the parlor talking to Clarence when

I came downstairs. Mom, either one of them could have seen me come out of that room."

Even though I was freaking out internally, I tried to keep my voice level. "I wouldn't worry about it, sweetie. A lot of people went upstairs to use the bathroom. Going into the wrong room isn't a crime."

"Blevins was staring at me as I came downstairs. Well, at me and Nick, who was waiting on the landing to ask me out."

"Really?"

"Um…yeah. Just for coffee or something. But if Blevins was looking at me then, I'd only stepped out of the room like…a few seconds before."

"Cassie, if they look for the diary and don't find it, they'll probably just think Edith threw it out." I gave her a reassuring smile. "I really don't think it's a big deal. Was this the only diary you saw?"

She nodded.

That didn't exactly jive with what Blevins told me, but I nodded. There could be multiple diaries, I guessed, but the one he and Clarence would be most interested in was the last one, since it would give them more clues about Edith's state of mind. I'd have to find a way to get the stupid thing back into Edith's house, but if I told Cassie that, she was going to insist that it was her fault and she should be the one to fix it.

"Listen," I said. "Maybe we should keep this between us, okay? Ed would have our heads if he knew."

That wasn't entirely true. I'd never even heard Ed

raise his voice. But I was quite certain that he wouldn't approve.

"That's why I didn't want to discuss it in front of him," Cassie said. "I was born at night, but it wasn't last night."

I rolled my eyes. "You were born at nine fifteen…in the morning."

"You know what I mean."

My stomach sank as I looked down at the diary. I hated keeping secrets. Work secrets were one thing. I'd kept plenty of sources confidential when I worked at the *News-Journal*. But personal secrets were different. Joe had obviously been keeping secrets from me for years, and look how that had turned out. I really didn't want to start out a new relationship with Ed by keeping him in the dark about things. He deserved better than that.

On the other hand, it wasn't exactly *lying*. If he came out and asked me whether my daughter had swiped Edith's diary, I'd tell the truth. It still felt wrong, though.

"So…what did you tell Mr. Nick Winters?" I asked, mostly to change the subject a bit.

She shrugged. "He gave me his card. I told him I'd see if we had plans, because I hadn't decided whether I wanted to yet."

I wasn't sure how I felt about this new development. Nick had seemed nice enough, but Sam Winters was a snake. Either way, I knew better than to voice an opinion. Cassie and I had danced this dance before. She was never the defiant type, even as a teen, except on the issue of the guys she dated. While it was possible that she'd outgrown that tendency, saying something positive about a guy had always been the kiss of death. Likewise, if I were to say I couldn't stand a boy, she'd feel compelled to go out with him at least once, maybe twice, even if she totally hated him.

I reminded myself that Cassie was now a grown woman and fully capable of making her own decisions, even if I didn't agree with them. That's how this *adult* thing works.

Which was ironic, given that I was also planning to handle returning the diary she'd swiped. But that was different. She could wind up in trouble. And if I hadn't told her what Blevins said about Edith seeing ghosts, she'd never have gone anywhere near that funeral. She was trying to help me, so if anyone got into trouble for this, it would be me.

"Well, we definitely don't have plans, so it's up to you. Something didn't sit right with me about his grandfather, though," I admitted, even though I was a little worried that even that statement might be enough to tilt her decision.

"Like what?" she asked. "I mean, other than the fact that his memory seems to be slipping, and he seems a touch racist."

"Racist?"

"He said some guy was Mexican and a thief, and I'm pretty sure he was calling him a beaner when Nick led him back over to the chair," she said. "Nick cut him off, but I don't know what else he'd have meant."

"Oh, okay. Didn't quite catch that part." I told her how Sam's mood had changed, especially when I brought up Edith's finances. "He went from light to dark like that," I said, snapping my fingers.

"Could just have been a mood swing. Maybe he was thinking about something completely different. You know how old people can be." A slow grin came over her face as she said the last part.

"What is that supposed to mean?"

She laughed. "It isn't supposed to *mean* anything."

"I'm only fifty," I countered. "He has to be over ninety."

"Fifty and *fabulous*," Cassie added, as she headed for the stairs. "Don't forget the fabulous part."

"Where are you going?"

"To get out of these clothes and take a bath. Then I'm going to finish Ed's book. Just a few more chapters to go."

"Wow. That was fast."

Cassie paused at the top of the stairs. "Yeah. He's a pretty good writer."

I felt certain she had an ulterior motive for her hasty retreat. She was going upstairs to read, leaving me down here to do some reading of my own. Edith's diary lay in the middle of the table, taunting me. And as awful as it was that Cassie had taken it, there might be clues in there.

I *really* wanted to take a peek. But first I needed a glass of wine.

Or maybe two.

☆ Chapter Eleven ☆

SOMETIME AROUND MIDNIGHT, the dark clouds that had been hanging around all day finally decided to open up. Rain had lashed at my bedroom window for the past six hours, like a restless spirit trying to get in. Restless spirit pretty much described me as well. I'd spent about an hour before bed reading and then rereading Edith's diary. There hadn't been many entries. The leather notebook still smelled faintly new, and the first entry was on New Year's Day. That made me a little suspicious that she began a new diary each year.

It hadn't taken me long to realize that Blevins was right about one thing. Edith Morton *had* been a haunted woman. By what or by whom, I wasn't sure, but the diary entries told of things moving, of whispers in the night, and of visits from someone she called *the boy*, or sometimes *the boy with black hair* or *the dark-haired boy*. He was watching her. He was angry at her. He was sad.

The entry that interested me most was written a few days before she died. This one seemed more personal.

My dark-haired boy came to me again last night. I see him everywhere these days, maybe because I know my time is short. He stands at the foot of my bed, watching me.

Sometimes, he calls me. He never speaks, but I know it's him.

Only You. Unforgettable.

It's All Your Fault.

And it is my fault. I never told anyone what happened. Of course, no one ever asked.

I always tell him to go away. That I'm sorry. To leave me in peace.

But he never does. His dark eyes will follow me to the grave.

Everything about that entry made me wonder if Blevins wasn't right about her jumping. I just couldn't get past the fact that the odds of that fall actually killing her quickly were fairly slim. She seemed like a troubled woman, but she didn't seem stupid. I think she'd have found a smarter way to kill herself if that was her intent.

When I read the first few entries, I'd wondered if maybe she was suffering from an undiagnosed mental ailment. Alzheimer's, maybe? I'd written a piece when I was at the *News-Journal* that discussed the hallucinations and paranoia that often accompanied dementia. But the more I read of the diary, the less that rang true. Edith's writing was straight from the imagination of a Victorian gothic author. It was a somewhat rambling and repetitive tale, to be sure, but vividly written and error-free, recorded in a spidery but tidy cursive hand that I could never begin to replicate. You could tell a lot about people from their penmanship, and Edith's didn't suggest that she was crazy.

It occurred to me at one point that the diary entries might actually *be* fiction, that Edith Morton might have kept a ghost story bottled up inside of her all these years and only recently started to put the words to paper. But if it was a novel, it really didn't seem to be going anywhere. And I seriously doubted that she'd call the sheriff's hotline to test out her prose.

Her words followed me into sleep, and my dreams were filled with dark-haired specters and open graves and creepy old Sam Winters. I was glad when daylight, such as it was, finally arrived.

Still, I sat in bed for a bit longer, my knees pulled up to my chest as the rain hammered on and on outside. It didn't sound like it would ever stop, and I wondered how high the river was. The town had flooded in the past. I was nothing more than a toddler the last time, so I didn't remember anything about it aside from what my mother told me about watching cars float down the middle of Main Street like they were part of a rain-slicked parade.

Shaking my head to clear both the daydreams and Edith's diary from my head, I resolved to get on with the day. I needed to go into the office and begin putting Wednesday's edition together. And I also wanted to talk to Wren. After careful consideration, I'd decided to tell her about the diary. I wanted her opinion. She'd lived in Thistlewood longer than I had.

Maybe she could help me figure out who this dark-haired boy might be.

After I showered and dressed, I slipped quietly past Cassie's closed bedroom door and down the steps. She was still asleep, and I didn't want to wake her. There was nowhere she needed to be, especially on a day like this. She'd probably sleep until noon if left unchecked, and that was just fine. That's what vacations are for.

I put the coffee on before reaching for the can opener, much to the chagrin of Cronkite, who yowled as though he was approaching starvation. A typical morning. I gave him a quick scratch on the head and emptied a can of Friskies into his empty bowl. He sniffed it, decided he approved, and then attacked. Again, a typical morning, although he will on occasion, for no apparent reason, decide that he's not in the mood for whatever I'm offering. I suspect he's trying to get me to open a second can, thinking he'll get a double portion. While I have yet to fall for that trick in the nine years he's been with me, he seems to live in hope.

I took my coffee and went over to the sliding door. Even if I couldn't go onto the deck and bird-watch this morning, it seemed wrong to drink that first cup when I wasn't looking out at the woods. The yard was a sheet of rippling water as it rushed downhill and toward the creek just beyond the trees. Suddenly I was very thankful that I lived so high up. The cabin wasn't much, but it was mine. I wanted to keep it.

There was movement at the edge of the trees, the slight rustling that I'd come to think of as Remy's calling card. Sure enough, the cub bounded out like he always did. I smiled as I watched him frolic in the yard, kicking up water and mud. He looked happy. Carefree. For a moment, I envied him.

Where was my phone? I wasn't entirely sure Cassie believed me about Remy, and this was my chance to get proof.

I found my purse on the kitchen counter and fished my iPhone out from the depths, praying that it still had a charge. It lit up when I hit the button, so I went back to the door as quickly as I could without stirring up too much of a fuss. Cronkite was still devouring breakfast. If he knew Remy was just outside the glass, the little devil didn't care. Breakfast came first. Food before foes.

Sliding the kitchen door open, I stepped out into the rain. Remy didn't seem to notice me. Raising the phone, I quickly snapped a couple of shots. He circled a few more times, then retreated back into the woods.

Once he was gone, I went back inside, shaking the rain from my hair. I looked down to check my photography, but that's when my phone decided to give up the ghost again. Time to get a new battery. Or maybe a new phone.

But I'd gotten the picture. Or I was almost sure I had, at least. I'd charge the phone at the office and show it to Wren and Ed when I saw them. They'd both stopped by to visit when Remy was convalescing in my shed, and I was sure they'd be glad to see the no-longer-so-little guy all healed up and dancing in the rain.

☆ Chapter Twelve ☆

I'D JUST FINISHED TYPING in the last few lines of a bake sale announcement and was thinking longingly about a mid-morning cup of coffee. The diner was one possibility, but Wren usually had a pot brewing this time of day, and I was sure she'd be delighted to caffeinate me in exchange for a peek at the photo of Remy. Just as I was about to close my laptop, however, the bell rang, announcing an arrival. I turned toward the door with a smile, hoping it was Ed, although it seemed a bit early for him to stop by. Usually he spent the morning writing.

But no. My visitor was Elaine Huckabee, and five minutes later, I was still baffled as to why she was in my office, sitting in the chair in front of my desk, sobbing uncontrollably.

I'd already handed her several tissues from the travel-sized pack in my desk drawer, so I just gave up and handed her the entire package. I waited while she blew her nose loudly, *again*, then promptly picked up the wail where she'd left off.

Elaine was, to put it politely, disheveled. *Total wreck* would also sum up her appearance quite nicely. Her red hair hung in clumps around her face, unwashed and unbrushed. If she'd had any makeup on when she left her house this morning, she'd cried it all away. I was fairly certain she was in pajama pants, and the rose-colored sweatshirt had seen better days, but probably not within the past decade. A black windbreaker that seemed too large for her was on the floor next to the chair, in the center of a pool of rainwater. Elaine doesn't cry pretty, not that I do, either. Her eyes were swollen and red-rimmed. Every now and then, she would stop and heave in a long, shuddering breath, like she was hyperventilating. I was beginning to wonder if I should call an ambulance.

"For heaven's sake, Elaine," I said when the sobs subsided a bit. "Try to calm down so you can tell me what's wrong."

She hiccupped. I caught a whiff of gin and wondered how much she'd poured in her orange juice this morning. Or maybe she'd been up drinking all night? Her eyes were certainly red enough for that to be the case, although that could also be from the river of tears she'd been spilling in my office.

When Elaine finally spoke, the words came out in ragged snatches, punctuated by sniffles. "Can't stop… thinking about it. I keep seeing…that woman's body… at the bottom of the stairs. I can't…eat. Can't sleep."

She hiccupped again, making it clear that while she might be finding it difficult to eat and sleep, drinking was apparently going just fine.

"Sheriff Blevins…called me yesterday. He said it was to see…how I was doing. You remember how much…how much of a wreck I was…after I found her?"

I nodded, although it was clear to me that she was in worse shape several days later than she'd been the morning of the crime. Or accident, I reminded myself, even though my brain clearly had fairly strong opinions on the matter since it always veered toward the non-accidental explanation.

"He suspects me! I just know it." Elaine blew her nose again. "He thinks I killed that old woman."

Old woman. Something about the way she said it bothered me. Yes, Edith Morton had indeed been an old woman. Some might even say she was a very old woman. But it sounded callous, and I couldn't shake the feeling that Elaine was only upset because she might be under suspicion. She wasn't upset by Edith's death at all.

And I was fairly certain that she was lying about the door being unlocked. While it was obviously possible that someone else stopped by after Dean Jacobs delivered the mail, it didn't seem likely. He said that he'd arrived a little after ten, and I was at Wren's just after noon. If there were no other visitors, however, either Elaine or Dean was lying—and I found our neighborhood mailman to be a much more credible witness than the sobbing mess currently hanging out in my office.

But if Elaine had a guilty conscience, why would she come here? I'm the sole newspaper reporter in Thistlewood, so it seemed a bit like a lamb seeking out a wolf. Was it because I had been there the morning Edith died? Was Elaine trying to convince me of her innocence because she was worried about Blevins and needed an ally?

That seemed a little paranoid. But I wasn't sure what other reason she might have for spilling her story —and many, many tears—in my office.

The tidal wave seemed to finally be ebbing. Elaine blew her nose again and looked around the room with dazed eyes, almost as if she didn't know where she was or how she'd gotten here. And even though I was afraid my next question would trigger another round of water-works, I had to ask her at some point.

"How did you get into Edith's house?"

She stared at me for a moment, frowning. "Wh-what?"

I repeated the question.

Dabbing at her eyes, Elaine said, "I told you already. The door just opened."

I leaned back in my chair, wishing I'd thought to flip on my now fully charged phone's voice recorder while she was in full hysterics and wouldn't have noticed. My past decade had been spent at the editorial desk, not out interviewing people, and I'd gotten a little soft. Oh well.

"Do you know Dean Jacobs?" I asked.

Elaine eyed me suspiciously. "Everybody knows Dean. He's the mailman. What about him? What's he got to do with anything?"

"He was there that morning, too. When Edith didn't come to the door, Dean grew worried. So he tried the knob. It was locked."

I watched her face carefully to see if her expression changed once she realized there was someone to contradict her story. But she didn't even flinch.

"He's wrong," she said. "It was open."

"I don't think so. He seemed quite certain. Why don't you just tell me how you got inside?"

Elaine took a deep breath and stood up, glaring at me through red-rimmed eyes. "I'm leaving. This was a mistake." She snatched her windbreaker from the floor, slinging drops of water in a wide arc around her. "I should never have come in the first place. Mr. Dealey was *wrong* about you."

Her mention of my old mentor took me by surprise. I wasn't surprised that she *knew* him. She had apparently lived in town for several decades, and everyone in town knew Jim Dealey. But why would he have spoken to Elaine about *me*? While I'd actually been eager to see her leave a minute ago, that made me curious.

"Sit down, Elaine. You're upset."

She pointed a finger at me as she backed toward the door. "No. I'm leaving. You just accused me."

"I didn't accuse you of anything other than not telling the truth about the door. And you could have a lot of reasons for saying that—"

"Mr. Dealey said you were a good person," Elaine said. "A good reporter, too. I had something I wanted to share with you, but…I can see now that he was wrong. You're not a good person. You're just looking for a story, and you don't care who you hurt to get it."

She stomped out to the curb and got behind the wheel of a battered gray Kia. As I watched her pull away, I wasn't sure which was more puzzling—why she'd been talking to Mr. Dealey about me or how she'd managed to drive here in a state of hysterics.

☆ Chapter Thirteen ☆

THE RAIN HAD SLACKED off but refused to stop altogether. It dripped intermittently on my walk over to Wren's house and now continued to drum gently against the windows in her kitchen. I'd been so distracted by Elaine's dramatic display that I was halfway there before I realized I'd forgotten my umbrella. Luckily the brown hat Wren had given me was in my purse. I pulled it on and discovered that it was quite useful for keeping the rain out of my face. Wren for the win.

"I knew she was lying about something," Wren said once I told her about my conversation, if you could even call it that, with Elaine. "Or hiding something, at the very least. But you've already told Blevins the door was unlocked…"

"And he didn't seem to care. What I haven't told him about, however, is this." I took the diary out of my purse and slid it across the table toward her. "Edith Morton's diary."

"Holy moly…where on earth did you get this, Ruth?"

"Let's just say that Cassie did a little exploring yesterday at the reception after the funeral. Although she swears she found it on accident." I filled in the rest of the details, and Wren sat back in her chair, staring at the small book.

"Do you think Edith was actually being haunted?"

"I don't know," I said. "Blevins said she called the station multiple times. Always in the dead of night. And it really doesn't matter whether I believe it or not. The real question is whether Edith believed, and this diary makes it crystal clear that she did."

"Well, like I said before, I'm kind of agnostic on the whole ghost thing. Heck, I *live* in a funeral home, and I've never seen one. Never felt the slightest presence. My aunt, on the other hand, swore she saw my grandfather walk into the kitchen almost every morning for the first year or two after he died. He'd go over to the coffeepot and look at it longingly for a few seconds before he faded away."

"Oh my," I said, staring down into my cup. "That's so sad. Could you imagine smelling the coffee, seeing it, *knowing* it was right there, and you couldn't have any?"

We were both silent for a moment, and then Wren said, "Poor Edith. If she was being tormented by something—or someone, because I'm still not convinced it was really a ghost—maybe she did jump."

"Maybe," I said. "But even if you're eighty-five, there's no guarantee that throwing yourself down a staircase—especially from the landing—is going to kill you. It seems equally likely that you'd just break a hip or something, and then you'd be haunted *and* hurting. Edith might not have been easy to get along with, but I haven't heard a single person suggest that she wasn't smart. I don't believe she jumped, and the fact that someone is even suggesting that she did makes me *more* suspicious that her death wasn't an accident."

"What are you going to do with it?" Wren said, looking down at the diary.

"I don't have any choice, Wren. I'm not sure how, but I have to put it back. If Blevins saw Cassie coming out of that room, and they don't find the diary, he could put two and two together."

"We could just burn it," Wren said. "Or drive out and toss it in the river."

"I can't do that. This is sort of like…I don't know. Her last testament, almost. If someone really was trying to push Edith over the edge—either literally or figuratively—this diary could contain important evidence. I need to take it back."

"Oh, Ruth. You can't be serious."

But I was serious. Very much so, and I think Wren could see that.

"We're too old to play Nancy Drew," she said.

I shrugged. "Angela Lansbury, then. And it's *me*, not *we*."

"Oh, you *know* better than that, Ruth Townsend. If

you're going into that house, I'm going with you. I can't let you do something like that alone."

"No. Absolutely not. You can bail me out if I get caught, but there's no way I'm dragging you into this."

Wren narrowed her eyes. "If you don't let me go with you, I'll tell Ed."

"You wouldn't dare."

"Try me," she said, flashing me a smug smile.

I didn't think she would. In fact, I knew she *wouldn't*. However, I also knew there was no talking her out of going with me. If I pushed the issue, she'd simply follow me around until the deed was done.

"Fine," I said. "When did you get to be so darn stubborn? We'll just have to find a time when Clarence isn't home, I guess." I glanced out the window toward Edith's house.

"That shouldn't be hard. He hasn't spent a single night there since his mother died. He's probably staying at the cabin."

"Well, that's a break. So…we go tonight?"

"Tonight it is," Wren said.

"Great. We've made it through more than three decades as friends without sharing a jail cell. First time for everything, right?"

"Don't be silly. We're not going to get caught. We'll wait until midnight. Go in the back door." Wren laughed softly to herself as if she couldn't quite believe we were actually doing this. "No one will ever see us."

"Okay," I said as my stomach did a little flip. "How do we get in? Break a window?"

"I don't think that will be necessary," she said, walking over to the keyholder next to the closet. I watched as she ran her finger down the line and finally came to rest on one near the middle, with a flower drawn in red sharpie across the face.

"You have a key?"

"Of course. We were neighbors. Edith gave it to me years ago, in case there was a problem when she wasn't home."

I breathed a sigh of relief—possibly the first easy breath I'd taken since Cassie showed me the diary. "Wren, you are a lifesaver."

"Well, technically, no," she said. "They always seem to arrive at my door too late for saving. But I *am* a pretty darn good best friend." She slapped the key down on the table. "Tonight at midnight. Wear something black."

I rolled my eyes and laughed. "I can't believe we're really doing this. It will be like the old days when the two of us used to sneak out."

Her smile faded a bit at that, and so did mine. It had been *three* of us most of the time. Tanya Blackburn was the third musketeer in our little group. But she'd disappeared during our senior year without a word to either of us. Just packed up and left, apparently, although we'd both had a hard time believing that.

I squeezed Wren's arm. "Thank you for being my partner in crime." Then, as I reached for my purse, I remembered the other reason I'd stopped by.

"Can't believe I almost forgot," I said, fishing out

my iPhone. "I finally got a picture of our furry friend this morning. Look how much he's grown!"

Wren took the phone from me and smiled. "Well, would you look at that? Hard to believe he's that big when he wasn't much larger than Cronkite before the winter. He looks happy as a…" Her voice trailed off.

"What is it? He doesn't come near the house," I said in response to her worried look. "I never go down there, either. He's too big now. It would be much too risky."

Wren shook her head. "No. That's not what I'm looking at." She tilted the phone so I could see. "Who is *that*?"

At first, I wasn't sure what she was talking about. But when I finally saw it, my blood ran cold. In the background of the photograph, just behind the first row of underbrush, was the dark figure of a man, staring straight at my house.

☆ Chapter Fourteen ☆

I LEFT Wren's place in a total panic. She offered to drive me, but she'd already mentioned she had a consultation scheduled with the Moore family, who needed to choose a coffin for their terminally ill grandmother. That was hard enough without having someone call to postpone it. My car was just two blocks away, and I ran every step.

The image on my phone was surreal, far too much like one of those made-for-TV suspense movies. All I could think about on my mad dash back to the house was that I'd left Cassie alone there with a strange man staring at our house from the woods. Had the weather been decent, I'd have thought it might be someone out hiking who had stopped to watch a young bear playing on my lawn, but the rain had been coming down in sheets, and my house was nearly a mile from the edge of town. There were several acres of trees between me and the nearest neighbor on all sides. No way was he just wandering around.

I punched the button on my phone and voice-dialed Cassie's number again. Still no answer. Even when she's sound asleep, the phone usually wakes her. I can't count the times that I've heard her groggy, slightly annoyed voice on the other end when I've called and caught her sleeping.

Ed's number wasn't in my voice dial yet, so I had to pull up my recent calls. My fingers were shaking so bad that I nearly called the wrong number on the first try, and I had a close call with running my Jeep off the road. He answered on the fourth ring, just when I was about to give up and throw the phone onto the floorboard.

"Ed here."

"Can you come to my house?" I said without preamble. "Please?"

I heard him struggle to his feet. "Ruth? What's wrong? You sound scared."

"Yes. I *am* scared. I'll explain everything when you get there. I'm on my way home now."

The rustle of fabric on the other end told me he was already putting on his jacket. "I'll be right there."

"Please be careful, though. The roads are terrible."

And they were. Main Street was a shallow but swiftly moving creek. No one was out and about now. Most of the shops were dark, and I wondered if they were even open.

"Are you sure you're okay?" Ed asked.

"I'm fine. But Cassie's at the house, and I think we've got a stalker."

I hung up and dropped my iPhone into the passenger seat.

The image had been blurry. It was impossible to tell for certain whether the mysterious figure was a man or woman, but the build suggested male. I was surprised that Remy hadn't sensed him, but the watcher hadn't been any closer to the bear than I was. Plus, the rain had been coming straight down, which could have messed with Remy's sense of smell. The bear cub probably just hadn't seen him. I certainly hadn't. Thinking back to that morning, knowing that someone was hiding and watching me as I stood on my deck, I couldn't help but shiver. I had been vulnerable. Unprotected. Anything could have happened.

And Cassie had been there all day by herself. I hadn't heard a single peep from her.

Ghosts, I thought. Edith's ghost. *The boy with the black hair.* I shivered again.

The trip home seemed to take forever. I scanned the tree line as I turned into the drive. No one there at first glance, but the odds of the man still being in the same spot hours later seemed slim. And if he wasn't in the woods, that could be even worse. He might be inside.

I came to a screeching halt next to Cassie's little white Honda and was out of the Jeep before my legs had time to adjust to the muddy terrain. My feet went out from under me, and I landed on my bottom, the icy water soaking through my jeans. Scrambling up, I hurried onto the porch and unlocked the door, screaming Cassie's name as I stumbled into the foyer.

Announcing my presence was probably a bad idea if we had an intruder. I wasn't armed. There were knives in the kitchen, though, and I headed in that direction.

"Cassie," I screamed again. "Where are you?"

Nothing. The only sound was the ticking of the grandfather clock across the room. Cronkite hadn't even come to investigate.

I glanced around the living room, looking for signs of a struggle. Signs of anything, really. The only thing I saw was my reflection in the silent TV, drenched, with clothes stuck to me like a wet glove. And then I noticed the basement door between the living room and the kitchen, standing wide open.

"Cassie?" I heard a rustle downstairs. "Cassie!"

"Mom?" Her voice rose up from below like a rush of warm air on my cold skin. I almost cried out in relief. "Down here," she said.

I hurried down the steps and found her crouched in front of the hot water heater on a blanket. Her headphones were on, and she was bobbing her head to the beat. I could hear the music from five feet away. A cardboard box was open beside her and a dozen or so photographs were spread out between her pajama-clad legs.

"I was going through some of Grandma's old—" She looked up and pulled the headphones off. "What happened? You look like the Creature from the Black Lagoon."

"I fell. In the mud. I've been calling. Why didn't you answer?" I tried to keep the accusatory tone out of my voice, but it was there, loud and clear.

"My phone is upstairs," she said, taking few steps toward me. It was almost like she was afraid to get too close. Like she wasn't entirely certain I was, in fact, her mother and not the Swamp Thing coming in from the cold. "I was tossing laundry into the dryer when I saw the box of photos. Sorry if I worried you. I didn't mean to be down here this long. But you go days sometimes without knowing where I am in Nashville, so…what's up?"

"C-come upstairs. I need some tea. I'll tell you up there."

"You get changed," she said, squeezing my arm. "I'll make the tea."

I agreed, mostly because my teeth were beginning to chatter. As I turned toward the stairs, something brushed against the back of my leg, and I almost screamed. Cronkite. He was wondering what was wrong with me, too.

The doorbell rang just as I emerged from the basement. Ed was outside and clearly out of breath. I could have hugged him, but in my current state that would have been a very bad idea.

"Good grief," he said. "What the heck happened to you?"

"Cassie's making tea. Let me get into dry clothes and I'll join you in the kitchen."

I toweled off quickly and pulled on my thickest sweater and dry jeans. By the time I reached the table, Cassie was pouring water into the mugs.

"I made you Sleepytime tea," she said. "You don't look like you need the caffeine right now."

"Good call."

Sitting there in the safe, brightly lit space with Ed, Cassie, and Cronkite, it felt like maybe I'd overreacted. I couldn't make myself look at the sliding glass door, though. First chance I got, I was buying some heavy blinds to put across there. A curtain. Something. Cronkite would be furious at me for obstructing his view, but he'd just have to get over it.

"Okay, Mom. What's going on?"

I reached for my phone. When I came up empty-handed, I started to go upstairs and retrieve it from my wet jeans, but then I remembered I'd left it in the car. And it was still pouring, so I opted to tell the story without a visual aid.

When I finished, Cassie looked a little pale, but it was hard to get a read on Ed. His face was like stone, and I thought it quite likely that he'd decided I was an irrational, overly emotional woman who'd dragged him out into the rain on a pretty shaky pretext.

"Well, I know one thing," he said. "Until we figure out what's going on, the two of you shouldn't stay here alone."

"Maybe it was just someone out for a walk," Cassie

tried. "He stumbled upon our house and saw the bear, too. Maybe he was afraid to move."

"In that storm?"

"Maybe looking for a lost pet…or something?"

"I left only a few minutes later," I told her. "You'd think if that was the case, he'd have flagged me down. Asked if I'd seen it?"

She nodded. "True. And it wasn't like the storm came out of nowhere. It rained all night. No one could have *accidentally* gotten caught out in it."

"Where's the picture?" Ed asked. "I want to see it."

"It's in the car. I forgot to grab my phone when I ran in the house."

"I'll go get it," he said. "I need to run back to the house anyway to pick up a few things."

"Why?"

"Like I said, you can't stay here alone." He gave me a sideways grin. "Yes, I know I'll have to sleep on the couch."

"No, you won't. We have a guest room. But you really don't need to do this. We don't know for certain he was watching the house. And I can't really think of a reason why anyone…would…be…"

Cassie and I exchanged a look, and I could tell she'd reached the same conclusion that I did. We both knew why someone might be watching the house. It wouldn't be Blevins. If he seriously thought Cassie had taken something, he'd pull up with the siren blaring, maybe even a search warrant. But Clarence?

"You said you didn't think it was a big deal, though," Cassie said hesitantly.

"What?" Ed said, looking back and forth between the two of us. "What's not a big deal? Maybe you could fill me and Cronkite in? Because we didn't get whatever psychic message the two of you just shared."

Cassie sighed. "Should we show him?"

"Sure. It's in my purse. In the Jeep. Can you grab my phone, too?"

Ed watched silently as Cassie pulled on her shoes and grabbed an umbrella. As soon as the door closed behind her, he turned to me. *That's his cop face*, I thought with a flutter of my stomach.

We sat there silently for a moment, and then he said, "You want to tell me what's going on, Ruth?"

I looked at him helplessly. "Cassie sort of…*borrowed* something from Edith's house when we were there yesterday. I think there's a chance that Blevins, or more likely Clarence, might be looking for it, so…I'm taking it back to Edith's house tonight. Cassie doesn't know that part yet, though."

"Cassie doesn't know *what* part?" Cassie asked as she opened the door.

"Why don't you tell Ed how you got the diary?" I suggested. "And then I'll tell both of you my plan. *Our* plan, I guess, since Wren is in on it, too."

The timer went off for our tea, so I went to the kitchen to pull the tea bags. I brought them to the table, along with the condiments tray and a little pitcher of milk, as Cassie told Ed the story—losing her earring, finding the diary, catching Blevins's eye on the way down the stairs. Then I told both of them how Wren and I were planning to return the diary. When I finished, Ed silently doctored his cup of English Breakfast and took a long sip.

And then he started to laugh. Not just a chuckle, but a real belly laugh.

"Wow," he said after a minute. "Just...wow."

"Ed." I touched his shoulder gently. "I'm serious. I'll be taking it back to Edith's house tonight."

He wiped at his eyes. "The heck you are. Not alone."

Cassie squared her shoulders. "Right. I got us into this. I need to get us out."

"No, no, no. We can't all go bumping through Edith's house in the middle of the night. That just increases the chances that we'll get caught. And I'm not going alone. I'm going with Wren...who has a key."

Ed scratched his beard. "So, what would you have me do? Just wait here? Let you and Wren go alone?"

A thought occurred to me. "You can be the lookout."

He gave me a *you can't be serious* look. "I don't do lookout. And I'm the one with experience in this department. Believe it or not, this wouldn't be the first time I've had to sneak into a building in the dead of night."

"I know. But you have to be the lookout tonight. I'm a little...um..." I gave him an apologetic smile.

His eyes narrowed. "Faster?"

"That's not what I meant."

Ed snorted. "Of course it is. And…" He paused for a moment and then rolled his eyes. "And you're right. You *are* faster."

Cassie was pacing. "Oh, lord. I don't like this."

"Calm down," I said to her. "It's going to be fine."

"Fine. Yeah, right. Exactly where do you want me to keep watch, Nancy Drew?" Ed asked with one eyebrow raised.

"Jessica Fletcher," I corrected.

"More like Lucy and Ethel," Ed mumbled.

I laughed. "You could be right on that count. Wren said Clarence has been staying at his cabin. Do you think you can find it?"

"Sure. We played poker up there once a few years back. Tiny place. We were crammed in like sardines. He used to be one of the regulars, but he stopped coming. Right around the time Elaine's divorce came through, come to think of it. His place is about twenty minutes outside of town."

"Can you make sure he's there? Make sure he doesn't leave?"

Ed grimaced. "I guess. But I don't like this, Ruth. You and Wren could get in trouble. Serious trouble, even."

"Maybe. But she has a key…so it's not really breaking and entering. We could say I was visiting, and Wren saw something. So we were checking it out like good neighbors?"

He looked at me doubtfully. "You think that'll fly with Blevins?"

I shrugged. "Why not? We're two middle-aged women alone. What else could we be up to? Anyway, we aren't going to get caught."

He stood up and sighed. I could tell his hip was hurting worse than usual. Had to be the rain. I felt bad for bringing him out in it.

"Let me see this picture," he said.

"So...you'll do it?" I asked as I pulled up the image.

"I haven't decided yet. Either that or I'll call Blevins and turn you in."

Grinning, I handed him the phone. The last thing Ed would ever do was call Steve Blevins.

Chapter Fifteen

MY WARDROBE DOESN'T EXACTLY lean toward goth. It's mostly jeans and sweaters. The only thing in my closet that was solid black was the dress I'd worn to Edith's funeral, and it wasn't something I could wear on a midnight caper with Wren. I settled on a pair of dark-gray leggings and a plain black sweatshirt of Cassie's, which was way too big for me. Too big for her, too, and while it was clean, it still carried the faint hint of after-shave. I had the strong suspicion that it belonged to a boyfriend, either past or present. Beggars couldn't be choosers, though, so I tugged it on, then grabbed a black stocking cap from the hall closet.

When I arrived at Wren's house, however, I saw that she had managed to locate a skintight black outfit. It wasn't leather, but there was definitely Lycra or some sort of super-stretchy material in the mix. I decided I didn't really want to know why she owned this ensemble. I was just going to pretend it was a Halloween costume. Some things you just don't need to know about even your very best friend.

"How do I look?" she asked.

"Like Catwoman."

"Exactly what I was going for."

"No whip?"

"I couldn't find it." She looked dead serious.

I placed my purse on an empty sofa beside the door and pulled Edith's diary out. "Are you ready?"

Wren took a deep breath. "As ready as I'll ever be."

I checked my pocket to make sure my phone was still there. "I just talked to Ed and Cassie. They'll call if anything changes up on the mountain, so my phone is on vibrate. He said Clarence's truck is definitely up there. Lights are on, too."

"I can't believe you told Ed."

"Didn't have much of a choice."

"Let's go out the back," Wren said. "Stay close to the fence. No one can see us from there. It's too dark."

We crept through the dark funeral home together, past the two viewing rooms and the kitchen in the back. Each step seemed about a thousand times louder than it should have been. I just wanted to go back home. Curl up with a bowl of popcorn and whatever was on Lifetime.

Wren opened the kitchen door just enough for us both to slip out into the night. I went first, and then she followed, gently pulling it closed behind us.

We were outside now. Outside in Wren's yard. Where I'd been at least a dozen times. Why did it already feel like we were doing something illicit, if not downright illegal?

The rain had stopped a few hours back, but the ground was still muddy. Luckily, Wren's backyard was high enough that it had escaped most of the pooling, but our feet still made a squelching sound with each step. We'd have to take our shoes off before going into Edith's house. Not good.

Wren had read my mind. Once we reached Edith's back door, she stopped on the stone patio and slipped her sneakers off. I did the same, scooting them over next to hers with my sock-clad foot.

Pulling my phone out, I checked the screen. Nothing from Ed, which was a good sign. Clarence must still be up on the mountain.

"Let's do this," Wren whispered.

Her eyes were dancing, and I shook my head in amazement. The girl was actually enjoying herself.

She put her key into the lock and turned it. For a moment, my stomach clenched. With my luck, I thought, the key wouldn't work. But there was a soft clicking sound, and then Wren pushed the door open.

The house smelled of Pine-Sol, so Clarence must have had someone come in and clean after the funeral reception yesterday. Wren glanced behind us one last time and then stepped into the kitchen. I followed, closing the door as quietly as possible. We worked our way through the parlor, and I stopped at one point, realizing I was in the exact spot where that creepy Samuel Winters had cornered me.

My dark-haired boy was back again last night…

Why had that snippet from Edith's diary popped into my head? I didn't know, but it sent a shudder through me, and I moved closer to Wren. "Cassie found it behind Edith's nightstand," I whispered, nodding toward the stairs.

I took point. When we reached the landing where I'd found the teacup, I paused and sniffed the air. Not whiskey, but an equally distinctive odor. "Do you smell that?"

Wren nodded. "Cigarette smoke."

I sniffed again. While I didn't remember anyone smoking at the reception, I suppose they might have. I wasn't a smoker and had never spent much time around one, but the smell was unmistakable. And it seemed fresh.

"Do you think someone's here?"

Wren shook her head. "Can't be."

We should have turned around then. But instead we continued up the stairs. I couldn't shake the feeling that we weren't alone in the house. Nor could I get the cigarette smoke out of my nose. Wren followed me so closely that we might as well have been joined at the hip. She was on edge now, too, which was unnerving given her nonchalant attitude when she'd unlocked the door a few minutes before.

We reached the top to find a long hallway with three doors on my right and three on my left. There was a large window directly in front of me. Pale moonlight, almost blue, spilled into the corridor. I turned left. The second door was open, and I could see a sink standing sentinel in the darkness. Edith's room, according to Cassie, had to be the one on this side of that bathroom.

I moved slowly toward the door, inching my way along like the woman in pretty much every horror film ever made, resisting the urge to grab my phone and use the flashlight app. Once we were in Edith's room, we might risk it, but not here.

As I opened the door, Wren reached out and grabbed the back of my shirt. She pulled me closer, whispering directly into my ear. "Do you hear that?"

I listened. My heart was pounding so hard in my ears that it was almost impossible to hear anything other than *thump, thump, thump*. We both stood there in the doorway, neither of us breathing.

A door at the other end of the hall opened.

"Where are you going?" a female voice asked.

"Downstairs," a man answered. "Be right back."

I swerved into the open doorway, dragging Wren behind me. We stood in the darkness and waited. Had he seen us? I didn't think so, but the possibility still made me very nervous.

"Hurry back, okay? It's kind of creepy here in the dark."

Clarence was *supposed* to be at his cabin. But he was here. With Elaine.

"I'll be right back, sweetie. Just grabbing something to drink."

His feet clomped downstairs, and then the sound faded away. Wren reached out and closed the door as quietly as she could, neither of us daring to breathe again until it clicked shut.

"I thought Ed said he was at the cabin?" Wren whispered in my ear.

My thoughts exactly. I looked down at the diary in my hands. The leather was slick with sweat. I crept over to the nightstand and knelt down, stuffing the book behind it. I didn't know if that was exactly where Cassie found it, but I didn't care. The job was done. Now we just had to get out of here.

"We'll have to wait until he comes back up," Wren said.

We stood in silence for what felt like forever, although I'm sure it was only a few minutes. Finally, I heard Clarence coming up the stairs.

"It's *freezing* in here without you. It's almost as cold as the cabin."

I sent up a silent prayer, *Lord, get me out of this and I'll never break into anyone's house again.*

"I turned the heater up, sweetums."

Sweetums? Wren looked at me and made a face like she was about to barf. I had to fight back a giggle.

But then he stopped. I couldn't see it or hear it, but I swear I *felt* his head turn toward Edith's bedroom. Then I clearly heard him mumble, "Thought that door was open?"

Wren grabbed the back of my sweatshirt again and yanked me into the closet. There was no time to close the closet door, so we pressed back into the corner. Something brushed my cheek, and I almost screamed.

An empty hanger. It hit me then that all of Edith's clothes were gone. If he looked inside the closet, there would be absolutely nothing to hide us.

The bedroom door creaked open. Clarence didn't flip the overhead light on, so I guess he didn't want anyone to know *he* was in the house, either. A thin beam of bright white shot across the floor. Probably the flashlight on his phone.

Clarence stepped in front of the closet—naked, but thankfully his back was to us. He stood there for a moment, and then, apparently satisfied with his half-hearted search, he headed back to the hallway, closing the door behind him.

Wren let out a shuddering breath and finally released my shirt.

"I thought you were cold?" Clarence said from the hallway.

"I am," Elaine said in a little-girl voice. "But I'm hungry, too. Let's build a fire downstairs and get some of those leftovers out of the fridge, and then maybe we can…" She trailed off suggestively. "You need to get your mind off this, baby. He can't hold that over you. You didn't do anything wrong. Heck, you weren't even in first grade yet."

"Doesn't seem to matter," Clarence said. Judging from his morose tone, I suspected she'd just managed to put his mind solidly *back* on his problems rather than the opposite. "Maybe I ought to just let them dig up the whole yard and be done with it. See what they find."

"Maybe you should," she said. "Then we could get some peace for a change."

"We should have left last year," he said as they made their way down the stairs. "She changed her will more often than the sheets on her bed. We're probably going to end up flat broke anyway."

"Now what?" I said once their voices faded away.

Wren sighed. "We can wait here, however long *that* takes. Or…" She glanced toward the window.

"You can't be serious."

But she was.

Chapter Sixteen

THIS WAS how I was going to die. Not warm and asleep in my bed. I was going to go out head over heels, screaming, as I tumbled from Edith Morton's roof.

Lord, get me safely to the ground and I'll never break into a house again.

"I hate you a little for this," I hissed at Wren as we climbed out Edith's bedroom window. It was only about a five-foot drop to the roof of the back porch. On a normal day, when everything wasn't slick with rain, this would be a cinch. But given the rain we'd had, I was more than a little worried that my feet would hit the shingles on a skid and I'd just keep sliding until I landed smack on the patio below.

But they didn't. I dug my toes in, feeling the wet shingles soak through my cotton socks.

Wren laughed softly as we began to inch our way toward the porch. "I've done a lot of things in my life, Ruth. But climbing off a roof is a first."

It was a first for me, too. I fought off a wave of panicked laughter, wondering how we would explain this if Blevins pulled up right that second. I couldn't think of any plausible excuse. I'd probably just slap the handcuffs on myself and save him the trouble.

When we reached the edge, I wiped my wet palms on the backside of my pants. The drop was considerably more than five feet this time, and I gulped hard.

"Not afraid of heights, are you?" Wren giggled. I was glad she was finding this so entertaining. At least one of us was having a good time.

"How the heck do we get down from here?" I asked.

Wren pointed to the gutter that ran down to the ground. It was bone white, shining in the moonlight. I sighed in dismay.

"Fine. Let's do this."

Getting over the edge was the worst part. I almost fell twice. Once I locked my feet around the flimsy-feeling aluminum, I let go of the roof and tried to shimmy the rest of the way. Halfway down, though, I lost my grip and smacked into the mud below.

I opened my eyes. My back was soaking wet, but I didn't think anything was broken.

"Ruth," Wren whispered from the roof. "Are you alive?"

I raised one arm and gave her a thumbs-up.

Wren had a much easier time than I did, but then she's always been a bit more athletic. She handled the descent like a professional cat burglar, sliding down lightly and landing squarely on her feet as if she did this every day of the week and twice on Sundays. Wren for the win...again.

We gathered our shoes and hobbled over to Wren's yard with them in our hands. No point in putting them back on. Our socks were soaked through. I just wanted to get back to the safety and warmth of the funeral home. And, yes, it might be the first time anyone has ever thought that.

The full impact of the cold didn't hit me until we were upstairs. I started to shiver at once.

"Let me find you some dry clothes," Wren said. "You can't go home like that. Hate for you to live through that ordeal only to die of pneumonia."

She got no argument from me, even though I knew I'd have to roll the sleeves and legs up two or three times. I pulled off my muddy socks and paced barefoot while I waited, trying to warm up. Clarence hadn't been at the cabin, but his truck was. That meant Elaine must have picked him up, but where was her car? I would have bet the entirety of my bank account that if I drove around for a couple of blocks, I'd find her Kia.

I sent a text to Ed telling him we were back and safe, but also noting that Clarence and Elaine had been in the house. Maybe one day I'd tell him and Cassie about the roof escape. I didn't even want to think about it right then.

He texted back immediately, repeating that there were lights on at the cabin, along with Clarence's truck. But maybe they were just a decoy.

What I didn't understand was why Elaine and

Clarence would have their rendezvous at Edith's house. Why not at the cabin, if they were still determined to sneak around? It was much more secluded up on the mountain. For that matter, why not at Elaine's house, wherever that was, if she was no longer married? It didn't make sense.

"Something just occurred to me," Wren said as she handed me a bundle of clothes. "The door *wasn't* open the other day. Elaine probably had a key, too. Clarence could have given her one."

"Maybe," I said. "Oddly enough, though, I didn't get the sense that Elaine was lying about that part. I asked her directly about the door when she was at my office, and she insisted that it was open. She's not a very good liar."

"Do you think maybe Clarence was there, too?" Wren asked. "The morning Edith died, I mean. Maybe he faked going up to the cabin, and he's the one who let Elaine in."

"It's possible. They both had a pretty solid motive for killing her," I said. "Not just the money, but...frustration."

She snorted.

"Get your mind out of the gutter, woman. Not *that* sort of frustration. At Clarence's age, they likely do more snuggling than anything else. But if Edith has been refusing to give Clarence his fair share of his father's money all these years, refusing to let him have a life, really..."

"He could have left town again," Wren pointed out. "Gotten a job. He had a college degree."

"True," I said. "Although at some point, I would imagine that having a college degree with little to no employment history starts to work against you. And I just don't know what to make of his conversation with Elaine. Who would be holding something over him?"

"Maybe someone who knows he killed his mother?" Wren suggested.

"I guess. But Elaine said he didn't do anything wrong. They didn't know we were listening. Unless he killed Edith and Elaine doesn't know it…"

"Yeah," Wren said. "And that bit about digging up the backyard. Do you think maybe Edith hid some money there? Like a buried treasure?"

"No clue. Either way, we can't do a darn thing with that information, because we can't say how we overheard it."

I changed clothes in Wren's bathroom, splashing warm water on my face for several minutes. The shirt she loaned me was something she'd been given at a morticians' convention, and the logo of an embalming-fluid supplier was now sprawled across my chest.

"That shirt looks good on you," Wren said with a mischievous smile after I joined her in the kitchen. "You can keep it. Consider it another little birthday gift."

"I like the hat you gave me a lot better."

When I left Wren's, I drove down James Street. Just as I'd suspected, Elaine's Kia was parked near a stop sign two blocks down. On a whim, I pulled off to the curb, grabbed the notepad I usually keep in my purse, and scribbled out a note.

I know you didn't do it, but I think you know who did.

When you're ready to talk, let me know.

I didn't sign it, since I was pretty sure that last bit would identify me. Once the note was tucked under her windshield wiper, I drove through the now-empty town, carefully sticking to the speed limit. If Blevins or one of his deputies stopped me, I was afraid I might spill the entire story. The only thing I could hope to win from that was a free stay at the county jail for sneaking into Clarence's house. I had yet to set foot in a jail cell, and I wasn't keen on starting now. Besides, Wren's embalming T-shirt would look absolutely tragic in a mug shot.

Ed and Cassie were already at the house, and it was nice to see my little cabin on the hill, cheerily lit up and waiting on me. It looked like home. I parked next to Ed's truck, casting a wary eye toward the tree line.

Ed met me on the porch.

"Different clothes," he noted. "What happened?"

"I fell in the mud."

He looked amused. "Again?"

"Yes. It seems to be a theme for the day."

Ed gave me a quick one-armed hug, and we stepped inside. The kettle was already screaming from the kitchen, and Cassie was placing tea bags in the mugs. She'd practically read my mind.

"One thing's for sure," Ed said gravely, "that won't be happening again. Even when I still thought that Clarence was up in his cabin, I was on edge. And when we found out he was inside the house..." He shook his head.

I thought of Wren and me inching sideways across Edith's roof in the full moon and gave him a grim smile. "You're right. No more not-exactly breaking and entering for me."

When I went into the kitchen to help Cassie with the tea, I could see that she'd been crying. I put my arms around her. "Oh, hon, what's wrong?"

"I was just so worried. If something had happened to you, it would have been my fault. I shouldn't have taken the diary."

"Actually, I'm glad you took it," I said, a little surprised to realize that it was true. Not that I'd enjoyed replacing it, but if she hadn't taken the diary, I wouldn't have overheard Clarence and Elaine. I had absolutely no clue what their conversation meant, but I was at least fairly certain now that Elaine Huckabee had nothing to do with the murder. She'd sounded far too sincere, far too worried about Clarence.

But Clarence himself? I didn't know. My uncertainty on that point was doubled by the knowledge that the shape in the woods today could very easily have been him. Admittedly, Clarence wasn't exactly a menacing-looking guy. He was in his midsixties, and while he seemed fairly spry for his age, I thought I could outrun him. But he could easily be armed, and no one is fast enough to outrun a bullet. I'm not a big believer in coincidences, so I couldn't shake the feeling that whoever killed Edith was also the person who'd been watching me on the deck this morning.

The dining room light was on above the table, and I felt completely exposed in front of the glass door. All I could see in its shining surface were our own reflections, sipping tea. Anyone could be standing on the other side watching. Probably not, since it was after two in the morning, but I still felt nervous.

"We need to drive into Maryville tomorrow and pick out some blinds," I said to Cassie. Thinking about it made me a little angry. Not the expense but losing the view. In the past, I'd always thought of the woods as my curtains, my protective shield around the cabin.

I gave Ed and Cassie the abbreviated version of *Wren and Ruth's Midnight Caper*, emphasizing the funny bits and leaving out the high-wire act. When I reached the end, I said, "So, I'm left with three major questions. Well, four, I guess, since we still don't know who killed Edith."

"Or even if she was killed," Ed said. "Could still be an accident, Ruth."

"Could," I admitted. "But I'm not buying it. Anyway, back to my questions. Why would Clarence and Elaine choose to sneak around at Edith's when they could have spent a peaceful night at the cabin? I thought at first that it might just be an in-search-of-a-thrill sort of thing, but…"

"What sort of thrill?" Ed asked, then cracked up when I launched into an awkward explanation. "I'm joking. You have no idea how many long-married couples I've caught in backseats or in the bushes at the park. Variety is the spice of life."

"So, you don't think that was it?" Cassie asked. "I mean, with Edith out of the picture, maybe they were sort of celebrating their freedom. Like having a house party when your parents are away."

"Is there something you'd like to confess?" I joked. "But no. They didn't seem to be celebrating at all. They were worried."

"I think Cassie and I might be able to answer the question of why they weren't at the cabin," Ed said. "After you texted that they were in town, we drove up closer. When we checked around back, the heating unit was completely torn apart. Looked like Clarence had been trying to work on it and then realized it was too much for him to handle."

"Oh. That's right," I said. "With everything else, I'd forgotten Elaine saying something about the house being almost as cold as the cabin." I glanced over at my fireplace in the living room. "Couldn't they have just built a fire?"

Ed shook his head. "Clarence *called* it his cabin, but it's just an ancient trailer that he built a porch onto. Very basic, very small. And since the lights were on, Cassie…um…took the liberty of peeking inside the window over the door. It's a dump, but someone has tried to fix it up. Make it homey. And since I doubt that would be Clarence, I'm pretty sure Elaine has been living there. When I got to thinking about it, I'm pretty sure Elaine worked for her sister-in-law, Gail, over at

Rapid River. You know, the tubing and rafting place? Managed the books, I think. Gail and Gary were always close, so I'm guessing that when Elaine's marriage ended, her job ended, too. So Clarence has probably been spending his allowance for the past two years—which, knowing Edith, wasn't much—keeping Elaine clothed and fed, unless she managed to find another job."

"So what were your other two questions?" Cassie asked.

"Who's the person holding something over Clarence, as Elaine put it? It sounds like he's being blackmailed."

"But apparently *not* for killing Edith," Ed added, "since that's not something that happened when he was a little kid. That means it probably has something to do with whatever it is he thinks might be buried in his backyard."

"But what could that *be*?" Cassie asked.

I gave her a nod of acknowledgment. "And…that was my final question."

"So let me guess," Ed said. "You and Wren are planning to sneak over there tomorrow night and start digging up the yard."

"Oh, no. I think we're done with that sort of adventure. But we do have an approximate time frame—about sixty years ago, since Clarence was still a kindergartner. And since his father had already left town, whatever happened must be connected to Edith. So, I *am* going to start digging, but for information. And I'm going to enlist the help of my lovely and talented daughter."

"I doubt we're going to find much on Google," Cassie said. "Not from that far back."

"You're right. But even before Google, we had these things called newspapers. I actually own one, come to think of it. And newspapers have archives. Think of it as a treasure hunt."

She groaned. "Are they even indexed?"

"Nope. Where's the fun in that?"

☆ Chapter Seventeen ☆

THE NEXT MORNING came much sooner than I'd have liked, given that it was getting close to dawn when we finally made it to bed. I opened my eyes to bright sunlight spilling in through my bedroom window and the sounds of someone, Cassie probably, moving around in the bathroom next door. Someone was definitely up already, because I smelled coffee.

I sat up slowly, fully expecting my body to cry out with all kinds of twinges and pains from the night before. Even though I'd felt fine when I went to bed, it sometimes takes a night's rest to uncover the damage done to your body the day before. But there was nothing more than a touch of stiffness, and that sometimes hit me just from moving things around down at the office. I stood up and stretched. Time to get the day started.

Opening my bedroom door, I almost collided into Cassie, who was already dressed in jeans and a sweater.

Her hair was still damp, but I noticed she had applied a little makeup.

"You're up early," I said. "Are you heading out?"

"Yes. I'm going to breakfast with Nick Winters. He texted me last night and said he was heading out of town this afternoon. He'll be gone for a few days, so I'll probably be in Nashville by the time he gets back. I figured, why not? It's just breakfast. I'll meet you at the *Star* afterward, and we can get started on our *treasure hunt*."

I laughed, because I could tell from her expression exactly how much she was looking forward to it. "Hey, it will be fun. We can laugh at all of the crazy hairstyles and advertisements."

"True. I hadn't thought about that. It *might* be fun. Oh, and by the way?" She lowered her voice to a whisper. "Ed is a keeper. He really cares about you. You should've seen him last night. He was worried sick. And he also makes good coffee. I'm going to be late, though. Bye!" She gave me a quick kiss on the cheek, yelled a goodbye to Ed, then grabbed her keys and her bag.

None of us had slept long enough, but the dark circles under Ed's eyes told me that he hadn't slept well at all. The mattress in the guest room has seen better days, and I'd offered to let him swap with me or Cassie. But he'd insisted that he'd be fine. I suspected he was regretting that.

"You look tired."

"It was a late night," he said. "For all of us."

Cronkite hopped down from the sofa and started

doing figure eights around my legs as I poured myself a cup of the coffee. Then he meowed and parked himself by his bowl.

"That cat is a dirty liar," Ed said, laughing. "I fed him when I woke up. He pulled the same stunt on Cassie when she came down a few minutes ago."

Cronk gave him an indignant look and stalked back to the living room, so I'm pretty sure he followed the gist of what Ed was saying. I offered to make us some breakfast, but Ed said he usually stuck to coffee until later in the morning. Something else we had in common, I thought.

"You should go home," I told him as I took a seat at the table next to him. "See if you can get some rest. I don't think there are any watchers in the woods waiting to storm the castle, and I'm going in to the office anyway."

"This is my second cup," he said, "so I doubt I'll be able to sleep. But I do need to go home for a bit. Get a little writing done."

"I'm sorry. This is keeping you from your work, and you've got a deadline coming up."

He leaned across the corner of the table and put his hands on my shoulders.

"You're a smart woman, Ruth," Ed said softly, his voice sending a warm shiver through me. "Don't say dumb things. There's nowhere else I'd rather be."

And then he leaned forward and kissed me. A quick, gentle kiss, followed by a smile that spread slowly, lighting up his eyes.

"So," he said, shifting topics like that hadn't just happened, "you're doing research today?"

"Yes. We have copies of the paper in the morgue that go back to its founding." I started to explain that I meant the *newspaper's* morgue, which is the name for the collection of past issues that are housed on shelves down in the basement. But Ed was nodding, so he must have been familiar with that somewhat arcane term.

"I was just thinking," he said, "that you *might* also want to check with some of the women at the Women's Club. Edith was one of the older members, but there are a few others still alive who used to work out at the factory. Teresa Grimes, Patsy's mom, worked there before she married Pat and they opened the diner. She'll probably know if there are any others still around." He finished off the last of his coffee. "You're not thinking about confronting Elaine or Clarence, are you?"

I thought for a moment. "I'm thinking about it. Not Clarence, even though I'm skeptical that he killed Edith now. But Elaine was clearly wanting to tell me something the other day when she stopped by the office. I pushed too hard, and she backed off, saying Mr. Dealey was wrong. That I wasn't a nice person."

"I'm going to have to beg to differ with her on that point."

I smiled at him. "Thank you. But she was kind of right. I was being a little snotty about the whole thing with her saying the door was unlocked, after Dean had said the opposite. Do you know how well Elaine knew Mr. Dealey?"

"She worked for him for a couple of years. Part-time, back before Gail opened Rapid River. Gary was a CPA, plus he did taxes on the side, and she helped out with that. I think it was more a hobby than anything else. Elaine liked telling everyone she was a reporter for the *Star*, although I don't think she actually did any of the writing. I could be wrong, though."

"Well, that would explain a lot," I said. "But to get back to your question, I doubt I'll talk to either of them today. I have no idea how long it will take to go through the copies in the morgue, and I also want to track down Patsy's mom, so it's unlikely that I'll have time."

"Teresa might be working the cash register at the diner today. Maryanne usually asks for Sundays off."

"It's Sunday?" I said. "Wow. My days are starting to merge together."

He chuckled. "Yeah, they tend to do that when you stay out partying 'til the wee hours."

"I'll drop in at Pat's this afternoon," I told him, "since I can't go anywhere near the place until Cassie's date is finished. Although I guess she and Nick might have been going somewhere else. I didn't think to ask. I'll probably tell Teresa that Edith's death got me to thinking about the old factory, and I've decided to do a historical piece for the paper."

"Sounds like a plan to me." Ed took his empty coffee cup to the sink and rinsed it out, then grabbed his jacket and the little bag that he'd brought with him last night. "I'll drop by the *Star* when I'm finished for the day. And Ruth, please make sure your phone is with you, okay?"

"Yes, sir," I said with a mock salute as I walked him to the door so that I could lock it behind him.

He narrowed his eyes. "And make sure it's *charged*."

I was already ahead of him on that one. "It's next to my bed guzzling electricity as we speak."

"Good."

He climbed into the Silverado and started the engine. I waved and was about to step back inside, but he rolled his window down. "Oh, and one more thing? Try to avoid climbing on any rooftops today."

And then he drove off before I could ask how the heck he knew about *that*.

☆ Chapter Eighteen ☆

I'D NEVER REALLY LIKED HANGING out down in the morgue, even when I worked at the *Star* back in high school. It's possible that it was just the name, but the room was also covered in dust—both the normal dust that accumulates in rooms that haven't been disturbed and the special dust from the slowly crumbling newspapers in the binders that line the walls of the small basement.

There were exactly 117 binders on these shelves, each with the year written on the spine in black ink. The vast majority of the binders held fifty-two eight-page copies of the *Star*, one for each week of the year. I began a new binder when I published my first copy as owner and editor during the first week of January. One of the binders is only half filled, because Mr. Dealey died in May of that year. And even though the binders aren't exactly dirt cheap, there are five that are totally empty, for the five years since his death. I couldn't bring myself to just skip ahead. And maybe one day I'll have the time to go back and pull up the obituaries and other key stories that ran in the county paper, so that the *Star* remains a relatively complete historical record for the town of Thistlewood.

It took me a couple of trips, but I lugged six of the binders from the mid-1950s up to my desk where the air was free of particulates—although it probably wouldn't be by the time I skimmed through a few volumes and the pages started crumbling beneath my fingers. I needed to upgrade the morgue with some protective folders for these things. Or alternatively, as Cassie would no doubt tell me, I needed to digitize. And maybe I would at some point. Invest in a scanner and hire someone to come in and make all of this searchable with just a few keystrokes.

It was a nice dream, but for the time being, I was stuck doing things the old-fashioned way. I opened the binder for 1955, since that seemed the most likely year based on Elaine and Clarence's conversation, and began skimming. The toughest part was not actually the dust—even though I did end up sneezing quite a bit— but rather the tendency to get caught up in stories that weren't relevant. That was especially true when I saw Jim Dealey's byline. This was long before I knew him, back when he was in his thirties and his dad was still the editor. I couldn't resist reading in full a story he wrote about a murder that year at a fishing camp a few miles up the river. There was also a story about the "new" gym being built at the school, which hadn't seemed new in the slightest by the time I attended. A few help-wanted ads caught my eye as well. The garment factory had either been expanding in the 1950s or else they'd had a lot of churn in their workforce, because they ran an ad in the classifieds almost every week.

About an hour later, I found something that was both interesting and possibly relevant. Wedged between an engagement announcement and an ad from the drugstore, at the center of what Mr. Dealey always jokingly referred to as the *society page*, was a picture from the annual company softball game at Woodward Mills. Two teams, all girls, each coached by one of the sons of Reggie Winters, the factory's owner.

I could tell instantly which one was Samuel Winters, even with the baseball cap partially shading his face. His brother, Marvin, who looked a bit older, was a bit pudgy, with a wide, friendly smile. While I wouldn't have said Sam Winters was handsome, even back then he simply oozed the cocky, cavalier attitude that some women—especially, in my experience, the very young and not-particularly-bright—seem to find appealing.

He was quite the ladies' man back in the day.

Nick's comment about his grandfather echoed in my head as I looked at the two teams. The faces were a bit blurry, and so small that it was hard to make out any features, but there were roughly twenty young women, mostly in their teens or early twenties, half wearing dark shirts and half wearing light. I'd guess that many of them were either fresh out of high school or else dropped out early. Sam Winters struck me as precisely the type who would have considered his father's employees to be his personal dating pool, and I'm using the word *dating* in the very loosest sense.

The caption below the picture read *Brothers Battle it Out!* That seemed a little sexist to me, since all of the actual physical labor was being done by the girls kneeling in front of the dugout as they smiled for the camera. In the short blurb accompanying the photograph, Marvin was identified as vice president and Sam as general manager. This was followed by a list of names, including two that seemed relevant. The first was Teresa Strumm, who might or might not be Patsy's mother. Teresa was a fairly common name. The second, however, was clearly related—Mrs. Edith Morton.

There was, of course, nothing in the picture that I didn't already know, aside from the fact that Edith played softball when she was younger. I grabbed my phone and took a picture of the team photo so that I could check it out with Patsy's mom if I tracked her down later, and then I continued my search.

In an edition printed two months later, the classifieds yielded something that I almost missed. I'd only been scanning the help-wanted section, and this was under *Real Estate—Rooms to Let*. If it hadn't been roughly parallel with the ubiquitous Woodward Mills employment notice, it would probably have slipped my notice entirely. The address was 109 James Street, and it offered a room and two meals daily, with a private bath and separate entrance through the garage.

I was almost certain that was Edith's address, but I

pulled the map up to double-check. It was her house, all right. The mention of a separate entrance had me confused—and a little wistful, since a separate entrance would have come in very handy the night before. But I supposed the place might have been remodeled at some point since the 1950s. The same classified ad ran for three weeks and then disappeared in mid-September. Either Edith Morton had changed her mind about renting out a section of her home or else she'd found a boarder.

There were no other mentions of Edith or Wood-ward Mills until late December, when a story in the *About Town* section nearly caused me to spew coffee all over the page. In years past, the Woodward Mills holiday party had been held at the factory, but with the new high school gym now available, the company had decided to rent the place out and hold a sock hop. Three photographs—one large and two small—were included in the article. One was the obligatory group photo, showing about fifty workers seated on the bleach-ers, the vast majority of them women. The only ones identified by name were the occupants of the top row— Samuel Winters, now identified as vice president, and Marvin, now president of the company, so their father must have either died or retired that year. Sam's eyes weren't focused on the camera. They were locked on the woman seated just below and to his right—Edith. Another woman and two middle-aged men were on that row as well, probably middle management and other office staff. Below them, the next three rows were filled with young women, all in full skirts and bobby socks. The only other male was a dark-haired young man standing at the edge of the bleachers, looking a bit uncomfortable.

What caught my eye the most, however, were the smaller photographs, which featured two different girls dancing. I'd seen both pictures before. In fact, I'd seen them almost every day since moving back to Thistlewood. The one on the left was definitely Patsy's mom, because I remembered her pointing to it that afternoon when she gave me the guided tour of the diner's photo collection. And the one on the right, with her head back and smiling, was Edith Morton.

Had Patsy's mom told me that? Maybe. She mentioned so many names that day, however, that they'd all run together. Teresa Grimes had saved that photograph of her younger self, with her skirt twirling above her knees, for the last exhibit in her presentation. "And that one," she'd said with a little giggle, "is me, when I took first prize in the jitterbug contest."

I grabbed my phone again and snapped the group photograph, not really sure why, except for the vague hope that it might trigger something in the woman's memory. Then I glanced at the time. Nearly two o'clock. Wow. I'd been at it for over three hours.

Cassie had promised to stop by and help after her breakfast with Nick Winters, so I was a little hesitant about going over to the diner. But I wasn't even certain that they'd gone to the diner, and even if they had, a breakfast that lasted until two in the afternoon—more than three hours—probably needed to be broken up. If they were still there, I'm sure Patsy was beyond ready for them to clear out.

So, I dropped the phone into my purse, flipped the CLOSED sign on the door, and walked to the end of the block. I stood on the corner across the street from the diner for a minute and peered through the windows. About two-thirds of the tables and booths were full, which wasn't too surprising on a Sunday since a lot of people stopped in after church. Teresa Grimes was indeed working the cash register, just as Ed had predicted. And if Cassie was there, she and Nick had to be at one of the booths in the back. *Oh, well,* I thought. *If she gets annoyed at me for interrupting her date, so be it.*

I crossed the street and quickly scanned the booths at the back through the window. Cassie wasn't there. That triggered a tiny twinge of worry. Normally, I'd have simply shrugged it off, thinking that she might have decided to go home and change or something, but that seemed unlikely given our creepy visit from the man in the woods yesterday. While Cassie hadn't been as freaked out by the experience as I had, she was still unnerved.

The rational voice in my head chimed in to note that the weather was lovely. They might have decided to go for a walk in the park.

The irrational voice in my head, always a tiny bit louder and more insistent, pointed out that I hadn't trusted Sam Winters one bit when I met him. Two of the photographs I'd found in my research that morning included Winters. And while that was largely due to bias on my part, since I'd been looking for information about Woodward Mills, I didn't like the way he'd been staring at Edith in the holiday photo. Yes, Nick had seemed nice enough, but the apple—even the grandapple—rarely fell far from the tree.

I walked around the side of the diner to the parking lot out back. Cassie's Honda was there, which ruled out the possibility that they'd eaten elsewhere. I yanked my phone out and called her. No answer. It could be a cell coverage issue, though. My phone was at a measly two bars, and we shared a plan. So I texted her.

```
WHERE ARE YOU?
   ^^Note  the  caps.^^  Mom  is
shouting,        kiddo.    Answer,
please.
```

And then, realizing that I could be standing in the parking lot for quite some time before I got a response, I went inside to question Teresa Grimes, the Jitterbug Queen.

Chapter Nineteen

"JUST MISSED HER," Patsy said as I took a seat at the empty stool closest to the cash register. She was making a fresh pot of coffee, which made me a little suspicious that she'd seen me when I was watching from across the street. "Well, not *just* missed her, I guess. It's been over an hour now. I didn't know she was dating Nick Winters. He's a good-looking thing, ain't he?"

I nodded. "Dating might be an overstatement, though. She just met him."

Teresa was chatting about some TV show that I've never watched with a couple paying their tab. I glanced back down at my phone. Still no text.

"A good boy, too," Patsy said, shoving the freshly filled basket into the coffee maker. "Not every young man would quit his job as an attorney to come manage his grandfather's business."

The guy two stools down from me, a regular named

Jesse, snorted. "That boy ain't no attorney, Patsy. He's a paralegal."

"So?" Patsy said. "Same difference, basically. He works in a law firm, right?"

"But he ain't got a law degree. Those are the ones pullin' in the big bucks. That boy figures he'll make more in the long run sucking up to his grandpa."

Patsy responded that Jesse didn't know what he was talking about, employing rather colorful language that questioned both his intelligence and the legitimacy of his birth. This was par for the course with Patsy during the off-season. When the tourists were around, she was sweetness and light personified, as saccharine as the iced tea that flowed from her pitcher, and the harshest words that tumbled from her mouth were *dang* and *shucks*. The rest of the year, however, Patsy considered herself to be among family and under no obligation to censor herself. Having divorced one husband and outlived another, I suspected she was sizing Jesse up as a potential replacement. They argued constantly, about everything and nothing at all, but Patsy always seemed happiest to me when Jesse was on his usual perch at the counter.

"And he's prob'ly gonna end up disappointed. He might drive a nice car, but I bet it ain't paid for." Jesse nodded toward me. "If your girl is trying to land herself a rich one, she might want to head on back to Nashville." He chuckled at this last comment, and I gave him a withering look.

"She not trying to *land* anyone. They were simply having breakfast."

He snickered at that and said something to the guy next to him. It occurred to me then that Jesse—and quite possibly others—thought that Nick and Cassie were having a morning-after breakfast. Why hadn't I considered that? I grew up in this tiny little fishbowl, and I know how people can talk. I should have warned her. I'm certain she'd have responded that she didn't give two flips what anyone thought, and on that count, I say good for her. But it still annoyed me.

"Ignore that old fool, hon. You hungry or are you just in here for coffee?" My stomach growled right on cue, audible even over the TV, which was airing some sort of monster truck competition. Patsy laughed. "I'll take that as a yes. You aiming for healthy or happy today?"

This is her standard question for both me and Wren. *Healthy* means we're doing the soup and salad combo. *Happy* usually means the bacon cheeseburger and fries. I was too on edge for either of those, however, so I opted for a grilled cheese with soup.

Patsy always carries one of those little order pads, but I'd never seen her use it for anything less than a table of six. She just yelled "Jack with a splash" through the window to the fry cook.

I had no idea what that meant, but he responded, "Comin' right up."

The couple chatting with Teresa had finally left, so I

decided to make my move while my food was cooking. "Hey, Miss Teresa. You got a minute?"

"I sure do," she said. "What do you need, sugar?"

"Well, when I was writing up the obituary for Edith Morton, it occurred to me that there might be an interesting story in the history of Woodward Mills. I mean, there are a couple of articles online, but they just talk about the business impact of it closing down, and things like that. I was thinking more of the human-interest side, from the perspective of the women who worked there back in the 1950s. I went through and found some old photographs, and I was wondering if you might be able to identify a few of the people and tell me if they're still living around here."

"I might," she said, casting a dubious eye at the phone I was holding. "Hold on, though. Let me find my glasses."

Smiling, I tapped the top of my head. She laughed and pulled them down onto her nose.

"Well, I didn't have to search very far, now did I? Okay, let's see what you've got. I expect most of them are dead, though. Edith and me are two of the last—although I guess Edith's gone now, too. Maybe two or three others. And old Sam, of course." Her nose wrinkled, and I got the sense she didn't like Sam Winters any more than I did.

I showed her the softball picture first, and she beamed. "That's me," she said. "Right there. I got a triple, and we beat Sam's team, six to three. And ain't that funny. I couldn't have told you the score of that game to save my life before you showed me that picture."

When I zoomed in a bit, she scanned the other faces and names. There was a woman who lived over in Maryville, she said, who was still alive as far as she knew, and another who lived with her daughter over near Pigeon Forge. I switched to the photo from the sock hop, and she picked out one of the same women from the group on the bleachers. Teresa took her time, naming the various women, almost all of whom had either moved away or passed on.

"Sam Winters might know more than I do," she said as she handed me back the phone. "He prob'ly had addresses for most of the ones who quit. Too bad you didn't get your idea for the story before Edith died, because she knew more about that place than anyone. Although…you might have had a hard time getting her to talk about it." She lowered her voice. "Things didn't end well."

Patsy grabbed my sandwich from the window and set it in front of me.

I was about to follow up on Teresa's comment, but Jesse snorted again. "Coulda asked her about Clarence's daddy, too. Wonder if she ever told him the truth?"

Patsy snapped a dishrag at Jesse. "Hush, you old gossip. You weren't even alive then. What makes you think you know anything?"

"Know more than you do," Jesse mumbled.

"Well, you don't know more than I do," Teresa said. "And I say you're wrong. I *remember* when Edie and her husband moved here. Clarence was already two years old before she ever met Sam Winters. And no matter how much that man bragged around town, I don't think she ever gave him the time of day."

"She worked for him all those years," the man next to Jesse said. "Must have talked to him sometime." It was one of the only times I'd ever heard the guy speak, aside from the occasional *uh-huh* or *I hear ya* in response to some comment or question from Jesse.

"You know what I mean," Teresa said. "Sam Winters made time with any girl who would let him, but most of us were too smart for that. His wife came down to that factory at least once a week. All she had to do was snap her fingers, and there went your job."

Jesse was about to chime in again, but I cut him off. "But Sam was interested in Edith, wasn't he?" I zoomed in on the section where he was looking down at her on the bleacher below.

"Well, of course," Teresa said. "Sam was interested in anything in a skirt, especially a pretty thing like Edie. That's one reason his wife—what was her name? I can't recall. Anyway, I think that's one reason she knew Edith wasn't having any of Sam's nonsense. If Edie had given in, Sam would have lost interest and moved on to the next girl. He always did."

When she'd identified all of the girls she could remember, I asked about the handful of men in the photo. She only recognized Sam, Marv, and one other guy she said died years ago. Then I pointed to the guy standing at the edge of the bleachers.

"Who is this? He looks a lot younger than the others."

She gave me a little smile. "His name was Carlos. Sam hired him on to do some janitorial stuff. I don't recall ever hearing a last name. Edith would have been the one to ask about him, too. He was her boarder for a while. I think maybe she pulled a few strings to get him that job because Sam…well, he never much cared for foreigners, and Carlos wasn't from around here. Obviously. Nice boy, though. I never believed what Sam said about him."

"What exactly did Sam say?"

"Said he was a thief. They had a big fight about it maybe a week after that sock hop. I didn't see the fight, but one of the girls who was working overtime that week did. Next day, Sam Winters had this cut on his cheek, and my friend, Della Shaw, said Carlos must have punched Sam a good one, because she saw little specks of blood under the warping machine."

"Warping machine?" I asked.

"Yeah. Big old thing that pulled yarn from one end to the other. Google it when you get home. I bet you'll find pictures."

I took a bite of my sandwich to hide the fact that I was fighting off laughter. It was kind of weird having an octogenarian telling me to google something. "Did your friend report it?"

"Sure did. Reported it to the front office as soon as we went on break. That was the first and only time I ever remember Sam Winters shutting the line down early. Closed the door right in our faces. And that was the last we saw of Carlos."

Suddenly the sandwich didn't seem very appetizing. "What do you think happened to him?"

"I think Sam Winters ran him out of town. He had to have been embarrassed that the boy beat him up so bad—I don't think the kid was even eighteen. Probably wasn't here legal, either, so Sam might have threatened to call the cops on him." She giggled, and then frowned at my reaction. "I'm not laughing about that poor boy. It was awful that he got sacked, although I guess that's what usually happens when you punch your boss. I was just remembering how depressed the girls on the line were for the next few weeks. None of them would actually have *dated* Carlos—that just wasn't done back then —but they all gave him the eye when he walked past, and I'm guessing a whole lot of them had fantasies where he was their dashing Latin lover. Not me," she added primly. "I was already dating Patsy's dad. In fact, that's my Patrick dancing the jitterbug with me in the photograph. We practiced for weeks because I knew Edith was gonna be hard to beat. I could dance circles around Edie Morton, but she had a better partner. Poor Patrick had to work at it. We won, though. Ten whole dollars, and that was back when ten bucks wasn't chicken scratch."

I looked up at the poster-sized photograph on the right. You could just barely see the guy in the picture with her. The photographer, almost certainly Jim Dealey, had focused his camera on the girls in both of the two dance shots, leaving their partners shrouded in shadow. Edith's dance partner wasn't even fully in the shot—just one foot and the hand that was holding hers as she spun out.

"So, who was dancing with Edith?"

She looked a little surprised, and then stared up at the poster on the back wall. "Well, if that don't beat all. Ain't it funny how your memory fills in the blanks? But you really *can't* see him in that shot, I guess, unless you already know. Edie's partner was Carlos."

"And you're sure this was just before the fight you mentioned?"

Teresa nodded emphatically, bobbing her silver curls up and down. "The big star they always put up at Christmas was on top of the factory roof. I don't remember the exact day, though. It's been more than fifty years. Hold on, Shelly. I'm coming," she said to the woman approaching the cash register.

It had actually been well over sixty years, but I didn't argue the point.

"And you're sure he left town?" I asked.

"Well, yes," she said, giving me a confused look. "Thistlewood's a small town. If Carlos hadn't left, someone would have seen him."

Not necessarily, I thought.

Chapter Twenty

WREN WALKED into the diner just as I was finishing up my lunch. We moved to our usual table at the back, and I checked my messages. Still nothing.

"You're worried about Cassie?" Wren asked.

I nodded. That was definitely the thing troubling me most, although my suspicions about the whereabouts of a young man who might not actually have left Thistlewood in 1955 were gnawing away at my brain as well.

"Cassie's car is in the lot," I said. "She was supposed to come by the *Star* and help me go through the archives. It's been close to *four hours*, Wren."

"The weather's really nice, you know. They could have gone on a walk or a drive up in the mountains."

"Maybe," I admitted. "But Cassie said the whole reason they decided to have breakfast instead of coffee or lunch was because Nick was going out of town this afternoon."

Wren shrugged, but there was a tiny frown of worry on her face, too. "Maybe they hit it off. You know what it's like. Some first dates, you can't get home fast enough. Others, the time simply flies."

"I've had exactly one date in the past three decades," I said. "You're more the expert on that front that I am."

Wren was married for six months when she was in her twenties, and frequently jokes that it was just long enough for her to learn not to repeat the mistake. She's had some very interesting romances, however.

Patsy dropped off Wren's pie with two forks, because she knows us. "You two are thick as thieves over here," she said, chuckling as she topped off my coffee.

I thanked her, then lowered my voice to a whisper as she walked away. "If it wasn't for seeing that guy in the woods yesterday, I wouldn't be so worried."

"Do you still think it might have been Clarence?" Wren asked.

"I did...until a few minutes ago. He had motive, and most likely opportunity as well. And Cassie said he and Blevins both saw her coming out of the bedroom. If he thinks she has that diary..."

"We should just tell Clarence the truth," Wren said. "We didn't steal anything, and we didn't break in, technically speaking, because I had a key. The most we did was dent a few shingles on his roof, but nobody knows about that."

"True." I decided not to mention Ed's comment about that until I had a chance to find out exactly where he'd gotten the information. "But again, I'm less convinced now. Remember how you said it might be a treasure being buried back there? Well, now I'm thinking maybe it's *not* a treasure."

Her eyes widened as I filled in the details I'd learned over the past few hours. She glanced up at the photograph hanging over our booth. "Do you think Sam Winters killed him?"

"I don't know. But I definitely think we have enough that it might be time to—"

"Incoming," Wren said, glancing pointedly at the diner's chrome ceiling. In the reflection, I saw Clarence Morton coming through the door. In and of itself, that wasn't unusual. Half the town walked through that door on any given day. But Clarence was making a beeline for our table, and the man did *not* look happy.

He slapped his hands down on the table in front of me.

"Hello, Clarence," Wren said in her most comforting voice. "Are you doing okay?"

"I'd be doing a lot better if *someone* would stay out of my business," he said, clearly directing his words at me.

He just lost his mother, I reminded myself. *Cut him some slack.* I still didn't particularly care for his attitude, however, or for the fact that he was causing a scene in public. There were only about a dozen people in the restaurant, aside from me and Wren, but I could feel their eyes homing in on our booth like miniature laser beams.

"You need to leave Elaine alone," he said. "She hasn't done anything."

Wren gave me a nervous look. I was pretty sure that this outburst was connected to the note I'd left on Elaine's windshield last night, but Wren didn't know about that. I crossed my fingers that she didn't accidentally blurt out something about our sneaking into his house.

"Clarence," I started, "sit down, please. People are watching."

He didn't look around, and he didn't lower his voice. "I don't care. Let them look. Let them *talk*. You can't stop people from talking. It's just what they *do*. I've spent my whole life paying way too much attention to what the people in this town think. Worrying about what they might say. That's all my mother could think of…and it wrecked her life and wasted mine. Elaine and I love each other. We're going to spend the years we have left together, and anyone who doesn't like it can go suck an egg."

Patsy, who was standing behind the counter, began to clap. Most of the people in the diner followed suit, and Jesse let out a long, loud whistle. I was tempted to join them, but there was still a part of me that wondered whether this was an act on Clarence's part. Judging from his reaction to the applause, however, my suspicions were off base. He stared at the table for a moment, then looked around the diner, clearly stunned by their support. There was one couple at a booth near the front who looked annoyed, but they may just have been irritated at the noise. Or maybe they were friends of Elaine's ex-husband.

"Clarence," I said softly. "Elaine sought me out. She stopped by the *Star* the other day. And she was really upset. I...I got the sense that she was worried about you. Or at least, worried about someone. She wasn't very specific."

It was true. I *had* gotten the sense that she was worried about him. But it had been from listening to their conversation last night, hiding with Wren in that dark bedroom, not from anything she'd told me when she was at the office.

"Elaine was just upset after finding my mother," he said in a defensive tone. "And yeah, I've been on edge about it, too. I'm not going to pretend she was easy to live with, and she was as selfish as the day is long. It only got worse once she started seeing things earlier this year. Plus, she was rotten to Elaine. But she was still my mom, you know? It was tough losing her like that."

I exchanged a glance with Wren. He seemed sincere to me, and I could tell that she thought the same. But I was still wondering what had the guy so worried. It could partly be concern that Edith had written him out of her will, but that didn't explain his comments about digging up the backyard. I was trying to think of a way to broach that subject when my phone buzzed.

Cassie's name and picture popped up on the screen.

"Sweetie, where are you?" I said, flagging Patsy for my check. "I waited for you at—"

"Mom?" She was trying to keep her tone light, but I could tell that she was scared.

"Where are you?" I repeated. "What's wrong?"

"I'm back at the house. Do you know what happened to that little black book I was reading?"

My head was spinning. She'd been reading Ed's book, but the cover was dark green, not black.

"The one that I had in my *purse*?" she added. "Did I leave it in your car? Or maybe at your office?"

Oh. She means the diary.

"It's in the backseat. I'll head home now."

The voice that spoke next wasn't Cassie's.

"That's very good, Ms. Townsend. I'll trade you Edith's diary for your daughter. Make sure you're alone, and don't mention this to *anyone*. Are we clear?"

Wren and Clarence were both staring at me, open-mouthed. I was pretty sure both of them had picked up on most of the conversation.

"We're clear," I hissed. "If you hurt her…"

"My grandson is a bit on the…impetuous side, but if you follow my directions, perhaps we can finish up this bit of business without anyone getting hurt." And then Sam Winters ended the call.

I threw a ten on the table and hurried to the door. Wren and Clarence followed behind me. Patting my pockets, I realized the keys to my Jeep were in the office.

"Why does Sam Winters think your daughter has my mother's diary?" Clarence asked as we crossed Main Street.

"Because she *did* have it, until last night, when I put

it back in your mother's room. There's a body buried in your backyard. A guy named Carlos, who I'm pretty sure Sam Winters killed in 1955. He was your mom's—"

"Boarder," Clarence said, huffing as he tried to keep pace with me on the sidewalk. "I remember him. He lived over the garage. Played the guitar."

I had actually been about to say *boyfriend*, not *boarder*. But since I only suspected the first part and the second was clearly true, I didn't argue.

"Did your daughter take all of them?" Clarence asked.

"All of what?" Wren asked.

"The diaries. There were like a dozen of them. I saw them in her room a few months back when she had the flu, but when we searched her room they were gone."

"Just the one." I slid the key into the lock and pushed the door open. "Cassie saw it under the nightstand when we were there. She knew I didn't think your mother's death was an accident, so she sort of borrowed it. And I really hate to ask this, but since it's the diary that Sam Winters wants…"

He stood there, staring blankly for a moment, and then realized what I was asking. "Oh. Sure, sure. Under the nightstand, you said?"

"Yes. Thank you. And again, I'm really—"

"We can deal with apologies and explanations later," Clarence said, heading for the door.

Wren gave me a quick hug. "Get the car and meet

us in front of Edith's house. She's going to be okay, Ruth."

Fighting back tears, I nodded. "I know."

"Who's going to be okay?" Ed asked from the doorway.

My face fell, and then so did his.

"You don't exactly look happy to see me."

Chapter Twenty-One

ED AND WREN stood on the sidewalk in front of Memory Grove, wearing almost identical expressions. Worried, angry, frustrated. I would've loved nothing more than to have both of them in the Jeep with me, but I wasn't taking the risk.

"Would you at least take a pistol?" Ed asked. "I have mine in the truck."

"I've never even touched a gun. So that seems like a bad idea. I'm going to tell him that you're supposed to be stopping by. Any minute. Maybe they'll just take the diary and go."

Clarence came running out of Edith's house, followed by Elaine. He handed me the diary. Elaine leaned through the window and clutched my arm.

"He killed Edith, didn't he? That Nick Winters guy?"

"Probably," I told her. "Either him or Sam, and I can't see Sam pushing anyone without falling himself."

"Nick sent a letter the day after the funeral. Said Edith stole money from his grandfather when she was his office manager. About twenty thousand dollars—"

"Elaine, I have to go."

She nodded and stepped back.

"Be careful," Wren said.

Ed leaned forward and pressed a kiss to my forehead. "Call me just before you get there. Leave the call connected. There's a recording app on my phone."

"Got it. Guess I shouldn't confess to any crimes while on the phone with you," I said with a wry smile.

"Hey, once a cop, always a cop. Oh, and when this is over, we will be rectifying that whole *I've-never-used-a-gun* thing."

No, we won't, I thought, but I just gave him a smile and told him I'd see him soon. We could have the gun discussion after Cassie was safe.

Three excruciatingly long minutes later, I called Ed.

"Okay, I'm pulling in."

"Be careful. I'll be listening. As soon as I can get through the woods from Ben Faircloth's place, I'll be watching, too. I'm guessing four or five minutes at most. I called Billy Thorpe, too, and he'll let Blevins know."

I hadn't believed for a single second that Ed would stay put, but it still worried me knowing that this was exactly what Sam Winters had warned me not to do if I wanted Cassie to stay safe. "Do you think that's a good idea?"

"On Blevins, I don't know. But he won't come in guns a blazin'. As for me, I've done this kind of thing before, okay? I promise you that I will do nothing that would endanger you or Cassie. Do you trust me?"

My throat clenched tight, but I managed to croak out an answer. "Yes. I do."

The cabin looked the same as always. I didn't even see the other car until I reached the end of the drive. A silver BMW was parked in front of the shed, with Nick Winters leaning against the hood.

Cassie was on the grass with her hands bound. With duct tape, most likely, because a piece was over her mouth as well. Probably a good thing I didn't have Ed's pistol. It would have been really hard not to shoot someone when I saw her like that, and I suspected I was not the only one armed.

Sam Winters sat in a chair, looking uncomfortable, although that might simply be because it was one of the cheap plastic stacking chairs I kept under the deck. I was a little surprised to see that Sam was the one holding the gun. It wasn't aimed directly at Cassie but simply pointed in her general direction.

I cut the Jeep's ignition, grabbed the diary from the passenger seat, and began walking slowly toward them. As I passed the deck, Cronkite startled me, jumping onto the table with a plaintive meow.

Cassie stared up at me with wide eyes. She'd been crying, and there was mud on her clothes from the ground, still wet from the recent rain.

"About time you got here," Nick said. "Give me your keys."

"They're in the Jeep." I held the diary out toward him.

"This thing is kind of a moot point now," Nick said, but he snatched it anyway and put it next to the roll of tape on the hood of the car.

"Not moot," Sam said. "We don't want to leave any loose threads hanging."

Cronkite hissed from the deck.

"Tell that cat of yours to get inside," Nick said, "or I'll kick him again."

Another hiss.

I dutifully told Cronkite to go inside and he, being a cat, ignored me. Nick reached down and picked up a chunk of rock. It wasn't much bigger than my thumb, but he had decent aim. It hit the picnic table. Cronk gave an angry screech, shot across the deck, and fishtailed through the pet door.

"You've got the diary now. If you and Sam are planning on making an exit, you should get a move on. Ed Shelton is coming for dinner. He'll probably be here soon."

"At three forty?" Nick snorted.

"We eat early," I said, narrowing my eyes. "So, did you sneak in *planning* to shove Edith down the stairs, or was killing her a spur-of-the-moment thing?"

That got his attention. Sam's, too.

"It was an accident," Sam said, although I could hear a touch of doubt in his voice. "Edith fell when she saw him. The whole plan was ill-conceived, which he'd have known if he'd bothered to run it past me first."

"Because Edith never actually blackmailed you, did she? I guess you could call it hush money, but you *chose* to make those payments because you felt guilty about Carlos."

Sam's thick eyebrows shot up, and he pointed the gun at me. "Should have known you'd be a busybody. Too curious for your own good. Sticking your nose in where it doesn't belong."

"You should put the gun down, Sam. Steve Blevins isn't the sharpest tool in the shed, but there's enough evidence in my office for him to put the pieces together. And I emailed the evidence files to three other people earlier this afternoon."

All of that was a lie, but Wren knew most of what I did. So did Clarence, and I was sure both of them would have already given Ed the details I didn't have time to share before I left.

Sam's hand started to shake. On the one hand, telling him I knew about Carlos might not have been the best idea. On the other hand, I had to let him know that I wasn't the only one with this information, just in case he and Nick decided their best option was to shoot me and Cassie before hitting the road.

"That boy's death was an accident!" Sam said. "I gave Edie Morton a job. A good one, too. Even took Carlos on when she asked me to. She repaid me by fooling around with that piece of Mexican trash. And then he had the nerve to tell *me* I was out of line in how I spoke to her. My own employee. In my own factory."

"We don't have *time* for this, Grandpa. Give me the gun."

Sam whipped the pistol toward Nick. "Don't you push me, boy. This is all your fault for being so greedy. You'd have had a nice little nest egg when I died. Heck, I'd have given you money now if you really needed it, and all of my secrets would have stayed buried in that backyard. I didn't mean to kill that boy. I was just going to turn him in, say he'd lied about his work status. Then he went and smacked me upside the face with a broom handle. I tried to get it away from him, and he slipped. Whacked his head against the warper."

"Enough!" Nick said sharply, and then his voice softened. "Come on. Let's just go, okay? If you want to do the whole true confessions thing, you can send her an email once we're safely out of here. Let's get you into the car…"

Sam looked momentarily torn. Then he nodded, and Nick went to help him up from the chair. I yelled out a caution, but it was too late. Nick ripped the pistol out of the old man's hand and shoved him back into the chair, which rocked backward, nearly toppling Sam onto the lawn.

Nick pointed the pistol at me as he backed toward the car. He grabbed the roll of tape from the top of the car and tossed it to me. "Tape his hands to the chair. Not that he could exactly chase after me," he said with a dark chuckle.

I ripped off a piece of tape and walked toward Sam. As I knelt down by the chair, I cast a quick glance at the tree line on the side of the house, which was where Ed would be approaching if he was coming in from the Faircloth place. The top section of the underbrush twitched to the right. Not much, though.

Could be Ed sneaking through the woods as backup, I thought. *Could also be squirrels.*

"I really am sorry about this, Grandpa." To my surprise, Nick actually sounded sincere. "You know this wasn't the way I planned it. All I was trying to do was get back some of the money you threw away paying off Edith. That way, I could leave you with a bit in the bank. But since everyone had to go and stick their noses in, I don't have a choice. You would just slow me down, so I'm taking the cash and the car. You'll still have your Social Security, and the house, and who knows, maybe someone will buy the land the old factory is on."

As I finished taping off Sam's arms, I saw Nick's shadow behind me. He yanked the tape out of my hands and shoved me to the ground. "You should have minded your own business."

Cassie cried out, but the sound was muffled by the tape over her mouth. I turned my head to the other side so that I could reassure her that I was okay. That this was all going to *be* okay. Her eyes were wide with fright, so wide that I knew instantly she wasn't just reacting to the fact that Nick had shoved me down and was about to bind my hands.

It was more of a look that said he was about to shoot me.

Chapter Twenty-Two

I BRACED for the sound of a gunshot, but instead I heard a roar as a giant mass of black fur hit Nick from behind. Nick made an *oof* sound, then stumbled forward and tripped over me. One arm flailed, grabbing at Sam's chair and knocking it over in the process. Then Nick face-planted on the lawn a few inches in front of his grandfather.

He'd managed to hold on to the pistol, though.

Pushing myself to my knees, I crawled forward as Nick tried to get up. But then Remy was back for another go. The bear swatted Nick hard across the side of his neck. Nick howled and fell onto his forearm, trying to angle the gun to get a shot at his attacker. I raised my leg and brought my foot down on his wrist as hard as I could. Nick's fingers flew open, and I lunged forward to grab the gun.

I rolled to my side, pulling the gun away. At that instant, Remy froze. His head jerked up, sniffing the air.

The bear met my eyes for an instant, and then he was off, tearing toward the woods on the far side of my house. Just as he disappeared into the underbrush, I picked up what his more sensitive ears had noticed a few seconds earlier—the sound of sirens heading our way.

A shadow was coming through the trees that separated my property from the Faircloth place. Ed was moving much faster than I'd have thought possible for a man with a bad hip walking over uneven ground. I suspected he was going to be feeling it tomorrow.

I scooted backward toward Cassie, keeping the gun trained on Nick, who was now clutching his bleeding neck with both hands. The cuts weren't especially deep, but I thought it quite possible that he'd need a few stitches. Sam Winters was still tipped on his side, arms bound to the chair, staring into the rear-left tire of his grandson's car.

Ed emerged from the woods, his phone in one hand and his gun in the other.

"What *was* that thing?" Nick croaked.

"I don't know," I told him. "But it looked a lot like justice to me."

"Well, somebody just ended her fifty-year streak of never touching a gun," Ed called out, giving me a smile as he raised his pistol toward Nick. "I've got him covered. You take care of Cassie."

I hugged her first, then pulled the tape from her mouth. "Thought you said Blevins was smart enough not to come in with sirens screaming?"

"Yeah," Ed said. "Apparently I underestimated his stupidity. Something he and I are going to have words about later."

The sheriff's cruiser screeched to a halt next to Nick's car. "What in blue blazes is going on here?" Blevins asked, whipping out his pistol. "Put the gun away, Shelton."

Ed, who was already doing precisely that, said, "Cassie here was out with Nick and figured out that he killed Edith Morton."

"So, it's a mother-daughter act now? I told Ruth that she needed to let that go. There's no…story… here…" He frowned, looking from Sam to Nick, and then he picked up the radio to call for an ambulance and backup.

"What happened to him?" Blevins asked when he finished the call.

I looked toward the woods where Remy had vanished. I wasn't sure how much Ed had seen, and later, I would tell him the entire truth. He already knew about Remy and had even seen the cub briefly one afternoon when he helped me look for the trophy hunter that killed the bear that I'm pretty sure was Remy's father. I didn't know if Nick had been planning to shoot me or not, but there's no doubt in my mind that things could have gone very badly if the bear hadn't acted when he did. And I was a little worried about the ramifications for Remy if I didn't lie my pants off. The man he'd attacked had almost certainly killed Edith Morton, but it was still a case of a bear attacking a man, and I didn't think the police would simply let that go.

Cassie must have been thinking the same thing. "Cronkite jumped him," she said in a shaky voice as I pulled the last of the tape from her wrists. "He's our cat. Nick threw a rock at him. Kicked at him earlier, too. And then he jumped Nick from the top of the car because he shoved my mom to the ground."

Sam, who was still lying on his side, said, "Looked a little large for a cat."

"That was no cat!" Nick said.

"I didn't see it," Ed said, peering at the scratches on Nick's neck, and then glancing over at me. "But Cronkite's part Maine coon cat. Weighs at least twenty pounds. He's feisty, too. Guess Nick shouldn't have messed with his family."

"You have an attack cat," Blevins said, looking at me. "Why am I not surprised?"

"It wasn't a cat!" Nick said. "More like a giant dog. Or a bear."

I laughed. "You think I have an attack bear?"

"Could the two of you put Sam right-side up?" Blevins said to me and Cassie. "And then somebody needs to start explaining exactly what happened."

"I had Edith Morton's diary," Cassie said, giving me an apologetic look over Sam's head, although I wasn't sure if it was another apology for taking the diary or for the fact that she was confessing it to Blevins. But she was right. We needed to tell the truth. I was pretty sure that Clarence wouldn't press charges, under the circumstances, and the odds of us being able to sync up the truth were a lot better than us syncing up lies.

"I saw the diary when I was at Edith's funeral…or wake, or whatever you call it," Cassie said, "and I knew Mom didn't think her death was an accident. We were going to mail it back to her son tomorrow."

Ed and I exchanged a look, and I knew he was thinking the same thing I was. Returning the diary by mail would have been the logical, sane thing to do. Yet it hadn't occurred to any of us—I'm guessing even Cassie—until that moment. Of course, if it *had* occurred to us, I'm not sure that I would have figured any of this out. And Nick might still have nabbed Cassie, assuming that she still had the thing.

"That's probably what we *should* have done," I amended. "But I was worried that Clarence might miss it. So, I borrowed a key from Wren and returned it last night. I'm sure you'll want a full, official statement from us later, but to give you the general overview, I believe that you'll find Nick has been using the closed-off entrance inside the garage to get into Edith's house on the nights that Clarence spends up at his cabin. I suspect he was calling her, too. Maybe even making her think she was seeing the ghost of a young man named Carlos."

"Carlos who?" Blevins asked.

"I don't know. He was Edith's boarder in 1955. If Sam kept employment records at the factory going back to 1955, he might be able to give you the last name. Or you could check dental records and DNA, because you'll find him buried in Edith's backyard. Sam can probably give you a precise location, although at this point, I think Clarence would be willing to let you just dig around until you find him."

"So...Edith Morton rented this guy a room and then killed him?"

"No. *Sam* killed him."

"It was an accident!" he said. "But no one would have believed that. A couple of girls on the line had overheard us fighting. He was an *illegal*. I gave him a job, the ungrateful whelp. No one even knew he was gone. No one missed him."

I glared at Sam. "Edith did, apparently. And you couldn't stand that." I turned back to Blevins. "Sam paid her hush money for years to keep it quiet. When Nick took over Sam's finances, he figured that out. He may have tried to get the money from Edith directly. Eventually, though, he settled on trying to see if he could rattle her enough to get her committed. But she caught him in the house."

The ambulance pulled in as I was speaking, followed by a second cruiser. The two EMTs spoke briefly with Blevins, then went over to help Nick and Sam into the back of the ambulance.

"Is that everything?" Blevins asked.

"Well, except for the fact that I think Nick pushed her. I'm sure he'll deny it. But I guess I'll let you figure that out."

"Thank you," Blevins said. There was a sardonic

note to his voice, so I'm pretty sure he was being sarcastic.

"You *should* thank her," Ed mumbled. "She just solved two murders you didn't even know happened."

"True. And now I've got all the paperwork to deal with, not just for Edith, but for a murder that happened more than sixty years ago. But, hey—you got your story, didn't you, Townsend?"

Shaking my head in disbelief, I said, "You know, that *really* wasn't my primary motivation, Steve."

I glanced over at Ed and Cassie. Ed was pacing around, shuffling his feet as he dialed someone on the phone. The foot shuffling seemed odd, but then I noticed something in the mud directly in front of me—a bear print —and realized what he was doing. I rubbed my shoe across it quickly, glancing around to see if there were others.

Cassie's eyes looked a little glazed over. I'd seen that look on her face twice before. Once was when she fell out of her treehouse and broke her arm in two places. The other time was at my parents' funeral.

"I'm going to get my daughter inside," I told Blevins. "She's just been through quite an ordeal."

I half expected Blevins to object and say that we needed to come down to the station immediately to give our statements. But there must be at least a small bit of decency in the man, because he nodded.

"Come on, sweetie." I wrapped an arm around Cassie and pulled her close. "You'll feel better once you're in dry clothes with a mug of tea in your hands."

"I'll expect the two of you at the station tomorrow morning," Blevins called out. "And you, too, Ed."

"Wouldn't miss it," Ed told him.

As the three of us climbed the steps onto the deck, he added, "Hope they don't inspect those scratches on Nick's throat too closely. Or the prints on your lawn. Because that was not a cat."

"Cronkite is big," I admitted, "but I doubt he'd have been able to knock Nick off his feet."

As soon as we were inside, I reached into my pocket for my phone. "I need to call Wren and let her know we're okay."

Ed shook his head. "Already taken care of. Texted her while you were talking to Sheriff Nitwit. You couldn't call her anyway," he said.

Glancing down at the display, I realized he was right. Completely out of juice.

"I just charged this thing!" I said.

Ed rolled his eyes. "Either spring for a new phone, or I'm going to buy you one."

"I'll chip in," Cassie said. "As long as you make it one of those cheap flip-phones."

"You mean the ones with extra-large buttons for seniors?" Ed asked, grinning.

There was no doubt about it. The two of them were definitely ganging up on me.

But I discovered that I didn't mind it one little bit.

☆ Chapter Twenty-Three ☆

THE SPRING I'd special-ordered to repair Stella had popped off again and was now somewhere under the printing press. I was lying on the floor trying to sweep it out with the handle of a broom when I heard the faint tinkle of the bell over the door. I'd already scraped a dustpan full of crap out from beneath the press. A few dozen ancient peanut M&Ms—Jim Dealey had been addicted to the things—along with a wide array of pens, paper clips, and type sorts. The spring, however, was still hiding somewhere in the depths. And now I'd have to answer the door with hands that were covered in a sludge that was part machine oil, part ink, and several decades of dust.

"Ruth?" Wren called out. "Are you here?"

"In the back!" I replied, relieved that it was just her. Sadly, she'd seen me looking worse. I swiped the broom under the press again. Something metal scraped against the concrete floor and I cringed. Hopefully the spring wouldn't be broken by the time I retrieved it.

Wren crouched down next to me. "What on earth are you doing?"

"Trying to fix Stella, but the new spring popped off. I think I have it, though." I pulled the next batch of debris toward us with the broomstick, only to discover that the metal I'd heard wasn't the spring at all. It was a large star-shaped earring, in candy-apple red.

"Well, I'll be!" Wren said. "Would you look at that? I remember those earrings. We wore them to the Fourth of July parade the summer of our senior year. Yours were red, mine were white…"

"And Tanya's were blue," I said with a wistful smile. That Fourth of July was one of the last times the three of us had been together before Tanya disappeared. "I never realized I lost the earring here at work. I just got home that night and only had one when I went to take them off."

"Talk about a trip down memory lane," Wren said. "Anyway, I just stopped by to see if you want to go get some lunch."

I pushed up from the floor, leaving a grimy hand-print in my wake. "Sure. Just let me clean up. Did you finish giving Blevins your statement?"

Cassie, Ed, and I had gone to the station yesterday as ordered and spent several hours telling and retelling the events of the past week. The sheriff's office had been busy with processing and interrogating the two

Mr. Winters, so they waited until this morning to get Wren, Clarence, and Elaine's side of the story.

"Deputy Thorpe took my statement," Wren said, "but Blevins did stop in briefly to yell at me. Did he give you the breaking-and-entering lecture, as well?"

"Of course. Which was stupid, since he knows full well that Clarence isn't pressing charges."

Wren smiled. "I don't think he's very happy about that. Clarence and Elaine gave their statements just before I did this morning, and Clarence apparently told Thorpe that if they'd had any qualms about me entering the house for any reason, Edith would never have given me a key. Oh...and did you know that Thorpe saw us on her rooftop?"

"Yeah. Ed said Thorpe was parked over on Main Street and could see someone was on the roof. By the time he got the car started and made it over to Edith's, the two of us were running into the funeral home. He called Ed to narc on us instead of telling Blevins. Which is a good thing."

"Definitely a good thing," Wren said. "I don't think Clarence put the pieces together and realized exactly *when* we were in his house. He might not have been so willing to let things slide if he'd known we got a nice long look at his bare bottom. I hope Blevins took it easy on Cassie?"

"He did *not*," I said, frowning. "In fact, he told her he could press charges for theft even *without* Clarence's permission, which I'm not entirely sure is true. She was already upset, and that just made things worse. I think that's what Ed was yelling about when he went in after Cassie to give his statement. He was still steaming when he came out twenty minutes later. Even told the receptionist on duty that she had his deepest sympathies for having to work with Blevins."

"Is Cassie okay?"

"I *think* so. She hasn't slept well since it happened, which I get. I was shaken after being at gunpoint for only a few minutes, and she was held for well over an hour. She seems in pretty good spirits otherwise, but she's going to wait on going back to Nashville for a few days. And she was definitely relieved when we found out that the charge against Nick Winters will be murder. Even if they argue it down to manslaughter, he won't be out anytime soon."

"What about Sam?" Wren asked.

"They're waiting until they have Carlos's body, although I don't know how much they'll be able to learn from it after all these years. I'm just glad they didn't check my place too carefully. We smudged the ones we found, but when I checked the next morning there were bear prints running all the way to the back of the yard. And speaking of yards, have they started digging at Edith's yet?"

Wren shook her head. "I saw Elaine this morning as she was moving her things into the house. She says they're supposed to start later this afternoon. Sam gave Blevins an approximate location, so she's hoping they won't have to rip up too much of their lawn."

"Clarence isn't selling the house?"

"Apparently not. They read the will yesterday. Edith left everything to him, with just one stipulation—that he didn't sell the house. His attorney said he could probably challenge that, but to be honest, it might be a bit hard to sell right now. I mean, there's this reporter in town who just published a story about a body being buried in their backyard for the past sixty years." She gave me a sly grin.

There have only been a few weeks when the *Thistlewood Star* was published on any day other than Wednesday. At Ed and Cassie's urging, this had been one of those weeks. The two of them chipped in and helped me get the story written up so that I could have the paper to the printer in Knoxville Monday night. I doubled my normal print run, and they were on shelves and doorsteps a day early.

I groaned. "Are Clarence and Elaine upset about the story?"

"No. I was joking! I don't even know if they've seen the paper yet. They just seem really happy. Like newlyweds…as I suspect they will be soon. Elaine was chattering yesterday about redecorating the house. Maybe taking a cruise." Wren gave me a perplexed look. "You don't seem entirely pleased about that. Do you still think Clarence was involved in any of this?"

"To be honest, I'm not sure. I don't think he wanted Edith dead, by any means, but anything that resulted in her being declared incompetent would have been really good for him. He might have been willing to work with

Nick to make that happen. One thing's for certain, though...if Clarence *was* in on it, Nick Winters won't cover for him. He was willing to hang his own grandfather out to dry."

I glanced down at my hands, which were as clean as they were going to get, but still ink-stained around the nails. I'd need to start painting my nails extra dark again now that I was back in the business.

When we got to the diner, Sheriff Blevins was sitting at the counter, chatting with Jesse. Patsy looked up and waved. "Ruth! I'm glad to see you. If you've got more copies, we're almost sold out."

"You're kidding!"

"Nope," she said. "Check the rack."

She was right. There were only two copies left out of the twenty-five I'd delivered that morning.

"I have extras at the office," I told her. "I'll bring them over when we're finished eating."

Blevins pushed his empty plate aside. "And there we have the problem with modern journalism in a nutshell. Always eager to cash in on tragedy."

Wren bristled, but I just laughed. "That's rich coming from someone in your profession, Steve. If there were no tragedies, no violations of the law, you'd be out of a job, wouldn't you? But people would still need the *Star* to advertise a bake sale or post a wedding announcement."

"Well, man, she's got you there," Jesse said. "Maybe we'd still need a school crossing guard to keep the kiddies from runnin' out into the street, but that'd be about it."

After we sat down at our usual booth, Wren said, "Blevins has got a lot of nerve. You're the one who solved the case for him, and he acts like you're some sort of ambulance chaser."

I shrugged. "It's like I told him when he was making the arrests. Yes, getting a scoop for the *Star* was a nice bonus. That wasn't the reason I was determined to find out what happened to Edith, though. I might not believe in ghosts in quite the same way that Cassie does, but if I hadn't at least tried to find out who killed her, Edith Morton would have haunted me. Maybe not in the literal sense, but she would have hung out in the back of my head, reminding me that justice had not prevailed. Now it feels like she's at peace. And maybe Carlos is, too."

Patsy arrived to take our order just as Blevins was heading out. "Hey, Townsend?" he called as he stood in the half-open doorway. I didn't answer, just looked up at him with a raised eyebrow.

"You two stay out of trouble, okay?"

"Can't make any promises," I told him. "I have a job to do. But we'll try to let you solve one every now and then."

Blevins didn't think that was funny.

But Wren did.

"I don't know about you," she said, "but I'm looking forward to getting into a lot more trouble."

Grinning widely, I clinked my coffee mug against hers. "That makes two of us."

☆☆☆

NEXT UP: A sneak peek at PALATINO FOR THE PAINTER (Thistlewood Star Mysteries #2)

Sneak Peek: Palatino for the Painter
(Thistlewood Star Mysteries #2)

☆ Chapter One ☆

ESTATE SALE
10–12 TODAY
EVERYTHING MUST GO!

THE HAND-LETTERED sign was barely visible between
the cars parked in front of the modest brick house on
Poplar Avenue. At least two dozen vehicles lined the
curb, with several more in the driveway. Lucy McBride's
home was only a few blocks from Main Street, so I
suspected quite a few people had arrived on foot, as
well. Small towns like Thistlewood don't get a lot of
excitement, except in the summer when tourists flock to
the area. It looked like half the town was taking advantage of this opportunity to snoop—and maybe pick up
a bargain.

I'd printed a notice for the sale in last week's *Thistle-*

wood Star, exactly as requested by McBride's son, even though I'd been tempted to tell him that no one around here would call the event an *estate sale*. Even when someone died, it was still just a *yard sale* or a *garage sale*, if you wanted to get fancy. Plenty of people would be snickering about how pretentious Kenneth McBride had gotten living off in California all these years.

On the other hand, given how far down we were having to park, it looked like he'd gotten an excellent turnout. Maybe he'd known what he was doing, after all.

Wren Lawson, my best friend, said, "You should take pictures of this crowd and post them in the classified section, with the caption *Classifieds Work*."

My daughter, Cassie, laughed from the backseat. "I'm not buying it. There are more cars here than you have subscribers."

I faked an offended look. "That's no longer true. I'll have you know we are officially in triple digits now. But to be fair, I suspect he pulled in at least as many people with the signs he was plastering downtown."

"True," Wren said as she craned her neck to inspect the cars parked along the right side of the narrow street. "I don't think all of these are locals."

She was right. Quite a few of the cars had out-of-state tags.

"Why would someone on vacation go to a garage sale?" Cassie seemed skeptical.

"Unless something has changed since the 1980s, Memorial Day weekend is kind of weird," I told her as

I pulled into an empty spot two blocks down. "It's warm enough that people want to be outdoors, but the river is still wicked cold. So while the crowds aren't nearly as large as we'll get at the height of the summer, there's usually decent traffic at the shops. And this is just a few blocks from the shops, so…"

Wren nodded. "The diner was packed earlier. Guess some of them saw the sign and decided to check it out on their way down to the river."

As I got out of the car, my eyes drifted to the house on the opposite side of the street. Nostalgia hit me hard, and I could tell from Wren's expression that she was feeling the same. The house across the street, the one with the now-peeling blue shutters, had been like a second home to us when we were teens. I think we spent almost as much time there as we did at our own houses.

Tanya's place had two advantages. First and foremost was location. She lived walking distance from both the school and the diner. While very little that would interest your average teen tends to happen in Thistlewood, anything that *did* happen, happened downtown. The second advantage was parents who didn't hover. It's kind of hard to hover if you're rarely home. When we were at my house, Mom stuck her head in every half hour or so to check on us or offer snacks. Wren and her brother lived with their grandmother, and while Gran Lawson was a sweet lady who made really good oatmeal cookies, she didn't have cable or a VCR. As long as we didn't burn the house down or crank MTV up too loud, we had the basement to ourselves, so we were willing to deal with the fact that the food selection was generally limited to PB&J and microwave popcorn.

"I'd forgotten that Ms. McBride lived so close to the Blackburns," Wren said.

"Me, too. But I'm pretty sure the only time we were ever there was for the graduation cookout."

"True." Wren turned to look at Cassie, who was getting out of the Jeep. "Last time we were at Ms. McBride's house, your mom and I were only a few years younger than you. We were rocking eighties hair, pegged jeans, and shoulder pads, and we were ready to Wang Chung and walk like Egyptians all night long." She stuck one arm out in front and one behind her.

Cassie laughed. "I've seen a few of Mom's pictures from back then. What were you guys thinking?"

"Thinking we looked wicked cool," I told her. "And we were right. It's not our fault that your generation has no sense of style."

A flash of movement at the Blackburn house caught my eye. Did Tanya's parents still live there? Were they even still alive? A curtain on the upper floor flickered again, almost as if to say that at least someone there was indeed alive.

Or, far more likely, the curtain had simply moved because the air conditioner kicked on.

"Do her parents still live there?" I asked Wren. As the owner of Memory Grove, the town's funeral home, she was also an excellent source of information about which of our citizens had passed away over the past decade since she returned to Thistlewood.

"Her mom does," Wren said. "Her brother, too. Bud moved away for a while, but he came back a few years before I did."

"So, did her dad die?" I asked.

Wren shook her head. "Or at least, if he did, he didn't die in Thistlewood. He left town a few years back. No one even knew he was gone for the longest time. He and Bud never really socialized much. Pretty much the mirror opposite of Tanya and her mom."

Sally Blackburn had worked part-time when we were teens, managing the books at her husband's construction company. She'd kept busy the rest of the week with her clubs and church, so she was rarely home. And Tanya had definitely inherited her mother's social nature. If there was a crowd, you'd find Tanya in the middle.

The fact that Wren and I were her friends had been the only reason we'd made it through high school relatively unscathed. Like many small towns, Thistlewood tends to group people into two categories—*from-here* and *not*. Depending on the individual you're talking to, *from-here* might mean you've lived in town a few years, but more often it means that both sets of your grandparents were born in Woodward County, if not Thistlewood itself. My own family moved here when I was thirteen, and that fact, combined with my stubborn refusal to suffer fools gladly, meant that I was suspect. Wren and her brother came to live with her grandmother a year later, and their primary fault in the eyes of many Thistlewood residents was the color of their skin.

Our shared status as social outsiders in a teeny-tiny school had quickly forged a strong bond between me and Wren. In ninth grade, however, for reasons I've never fully understood, Tanya Blackburn—who was definitely *from-here*—thumbed her nose at her social circle by carrying her lunch tray over to sit with the two of us. The whole situation was touch and go for a bit, as to whether the others would accept us or shun Tanya. Her total indifference to the outcome was probably what decided the matter. She made it clear that the three of us were a package deal, and the center of gravity in the cafeteria gradually shifted to what had been the outcast table. There were still plenty of snide comments about me and Wren over the next few years, but Tanya pulled us into her circle through the sheer force of her will.

And then one day, the summer after graduation, Tanya was gone. Just up and vanished over the Fourth of July weekend. Packed her things into the back of her car and headed to Nashville, her parents said, without so much as a word of goodbye.

I hadn't believed it for a second. Neither had Wren. Yes, Tanya had been planning to move to Nashville, but she was going at the end of the summer. We were going to rent a place together. I was starting college in the fall at Vanderbilt. Tanya had no interest in higher educa-tion—she was going to find a job and try to land singing gigs at night. And as tough as it is to break through as a singer, none of us ever doubted that Tanya would make it. She would be the next Bonnie Tyler or Pat Benatar.

Wren, who had wanted to be a doctor back then, had joined the Army to earn cash for college. Once her enlistment was up, she would join us in Nashville.

We'd had it all planned out. In fact, we'd been planning it for two entire years. So nope. Wren and I didn't believe she'd simply run off. But, unfortunately, we were pretty much the only ones.

Two men were carrying a dresser over to their pickup truck when we reached the McBride house.

"Got this for thirty dollars!" the younger one said to Wren as he sidestepped the realtor's sign, which now sported a SOLD banner. "Can you believe it?"

"Looks like you drive a hard bargain," Wren told him.

The man on the other end of the load, who I thought might be the younger one's father, chuckled. "I gotta teach you to haggle, boy. You should've offered him twenty. Pretty sure he'd have taken it."

We dodged a few people clustered around the open garage door and stepped inside the house. Wren suggested that we check out the upstairs first, since the drawer had broken on her nightstand and she was in the market for a replacement. Two of the bedrooms, however, were already stripped clean, and the only nightstand left had a note taped to the top saying that it had been sold to the people who purchased the house.

"Well, poo," Wren said. "Guess we should have gotten here earlier."

We wandered around a bit more, then went back down to the living room.

Wren smiled and ran her finger along the spine of one of the many books that lined the shelves of the living room. "This part of the house is so *very* Ms. McBride."

She was right. All you had to do was look around and you knew instantly what our former English teacher had loved most. If she wasn't standing in front of the class teaching, Lucy McBride's nose had always been deep inside a book. I once caught her hiding out in her office during a pep rally, which teachers were expected to attend unless they had some other pressing task. In her case, the "pressing task" had been finishing John Irving's *The Cider House Rules*.

Given the sheer number of books in this room, and on the shelves upstairs, I had the sense that she hadn't parted with many of them when she reached that final page.

Ms. McBride's teaching influenced my eventual career almost as much as my after-school job at the *Thistlewood Star.* Jim Dealey taught me the mechanics of reporting and the specific skills needed to run a small-town newspaper, many of which still came in handy during the twenty-six years I worked at the much larger *Nashville News-Journal*. Lucy McBride was the one who kindled my love for the written word and who honed my writing skills to the point that I tested out of freshman comp in college. I was her prodigy—during my last two years of high school, she entered my work in writing contests and sent me scholarship information for creative writing programs. I'm pretty sure she expected me to write the great American novel some-day, and she'd been deeply disappointed when I'd opted to write the news instead.

"The world needs more beauty," she'd told me the night our senior class—all thirty-seven of us—gathered here at her home for our pre-graduation cookout. "More poetry, more imagination. That's what makes life worth living. Why not write stories that lift people up? That make them happy? Do you really want to spend your entire career writing about tragedy and corruption?"

I'll admit that her words stung a bit. But I knew she was upset about my decision, almost as if it was a personal rejection. So I'd simply smiled and said, "The news is important, too. Someone has to write stories that explain the world we live in. And I'll do my best to sneak a little beauty into the mix."

We'd kept in touch at first, but the last time I'd spoken to Ms. McBride was at my own parents' funeral nearly a decade ago. I'd planned to look her up when I moved back to Thistlewood last fall, but it was one of those things I hadn't gotten around to doing during that first miserable month, as I went about the many tasks involved in ending a marriage of nearly thirty years. I'd also just purchased what was left of the *Star*, which had been shuttered since Mr. Dealey died five years earlier, and was trying to figure out what I'd need to do to get the paper up and running again. The answer to that question had been "a whole heck of a lot," unfortu-nately, which had left me very little time for social calls.

As fate would have it, Ms. McBride had passed away peacefully in her sleep by the time I got settled. I didn't even have the online version of the *Star* going at that point, so I hadn't been able to post an obituary for her. One of the odd quirks of my former boss at the *Star* was his belief that every person's last mention in his paper should be distinctive. Your obituary was your final bow, he'd always said, and it should stand out, rather than blending in with a notice for a community garage sale being held in the local park next Friday. So he'd given every person their own special font face— some bold, some italic, some serif, some sans. For example, the former high school football coach died right after I started working at the *Star.* Coach Bailey was an obnoxious little toad of a man who'd routinely yelled not just at his team, but at pretty much everyone. Mr. Dealey composed his obituary in Times New Roman, a perfectly ordinary and respectable font. But he'd used small-caps. It was a subtle enough joke that most people missed it, but those who got it had to admit that it was perfect.

I'd decided to keep that tradition going, and if I'd been up and running in time to publish Lucy McBride's obituary, I would have chosen a pretty font. Something flowing like Lucida Calligraphy or Edwardian Script. Her love of beauty was reflected in the house she'd shared with her son, Kenneth, until he grew up and moved to California a few years after I headed off to college. It was a colorful house—not in a garish way, but with walls of seafoam green and pale yellow instead of the ubiquitous beige most people adopt. When we first arrived, a cheerful abstract print rug had still covered much of the hardwood floor in the foyer, but a man was now rolling it up while his wife dug around in her purse for some cash. The news that they paid a mere ten dollars for the rug seemed to start a chain reaction, and people were coming up to Kenneth, pointing at various objects, and throwing sinfully low offers his way. I didn't see him refuse a single one. He just nodded, as if their offer of fifty dollars was perfectly fine for his late mother's nearly new leather sofa. Maybe he didn't need the money. It was entirely possible that he just wanted this all to be over so he could go back to the airport and catch the next plane home.

"I don't think Ms. McBride would like this," Wren said. "All these people milling about, touching her things. Sitting on her furniture. She was a very private person."

"I know. It's a necessary step, though, if you're going to sell the house."

"True," she admitted. "The only real alternative is hiding things away in storage, like I did when I sold Gran's place. I should haul all of that stuff out and have a sale of my own soon."

I'd donated most of my parents' personal items after their funeral, keeping just a few mementos. But I'd never had to deal with putting their house on the market, since Cassie and I—and occasionally her father —had always spent a few weeks here in the summer, taking advantage of the river and the nearby tourist attractions in Pigeon Forge, Gatlinburg, and Sevierville. And in retrospect, keeping their house had been a very good thing. When Joe had his mid-life revelation and decided he was no longer in the mood to be married to me, I'd been able to pile my clothes and a few other things into the Jeep and simply go. It was a relief not to worry about divvying up furniture, dishes, and so forth.

The only thing I'd really missed from my life in Nashville was my daughter, and recent events seemed to have solved that problem. Cassie had decided not to return to Nashville after our misadventure a few months ago, when Edith Morton's killer held us at gunpoint. I was glad to have Cassie home, but the decision worried me. She'd had a life in Nashville, and a job she enjoyed. Was she staying because she wanted to be here, or because that experience had scarred her. She *seemed* okay to me, but what was there in a tiny mountain town for a girl in her early twenties? How long would she enjoy weekend outings like this one, accompanying her mom and her mom's best friend to an estate sale? When I was her age, I would have been bored silly. There was no force on the planet that could have convinced a twenty-two-year-old Ruth Townsend to live in Thistlewood, Tennessee.

"Do you know where Cassie went?" I asked Wren.

"Still upstairs, I think." She leaned toward me and whispered, "Cross your fingers that she hasn't found another diary. I don't have a key to this place, so sneaking in to return it would be much harder."

"Remind me to check her purse before we leave," I

said. Cassie's curiosity was a large reason we'd wound up in hot water a few months back, but it was also a major factor in me solving the case. Not something I'd want to risk again, however.

Wren glanced over at Kenneth McBride, standing at the edge of the room with a dazed expression on his face. Human interaction didn't seem to be his strongest suit. Or maybe he just didn't like crowds.

"Oh, Ruth," she whispered. "Why did we come here? This is actually sad."

"I know. Do you want to leave?"

"Yes. But first I'm going to buy some of these books. I'll give them a good home. The ones I don't have room for, I'll donate to the library. How much do you think I should offer?"

"I don't know. Maybe you should ask him?"

Wren squared her shoulders as if she were preparing for battle and walked across the living room. I hung back, trying to stay out of everyone's way, and watched as she tapped him lightly on the shoulder. Her lips were moving, but I couldn't hear what she was saying over the ambient noise—a baby crying somewhere, laughter upstairs.

Someone stepped up behind me. I turned, thinking it was Cassie, but instead found Dean Jacobs smiling at me. As usual, he was looking very handsome, something that's hard to pull off in a mail carrier's uniform.

"Good morning, Ruth."

"Dean! It's so good to see you. What brings you here?"

He looked around doubtfully. "I'm kind of wondering that myself. Not like I need anything else cluttering up my house. I should have a sale of my own, actually."

"You should team up with Wren," I said and looked down at my watch. "It's early. Mail already delivered?"

Dean laughed but looked a little guilty. "Nah. Just taking a quick break. Saw the sign when I was coming down the sidewalk and noticed your Jeep out by the curb." He glanced down at the floor. "I was sorry to hear about what happened to you and Cassie. Can't say I ever really liked the two of them, but I didn't think they were murderers."

"Greed can be a powerful motivator," I said. "I'm just glad that it's over."

"Yeah. Me, too. Is…um…Cassie staying in town for a while?"

I nodded. "Yeah. I think she's at sort of a cross-roads. Trying to figure out what she wants to do next."

"Oh. Is she…here?" His face was turning red, and I laughed. I couldn't help it.

"You should come up and see us one night," I told him. "If not for you mentioning that Edith's door was locked the day she died, I might not have figured things out. The least I can do is cook you dinner."

He looked surprised. "Really?"

"Sure. Why not?"

"Do you think Cassie would like that?"

"I don't know," I answered truthfully. "I would, though."

"Then I'd love to. Just let me know when."

Cassie chose that moment to appear, and Dean flushed again.

"Good morning, Cassie."

"Oh, hey, Dean," she said, and then turned toward me. I wanted to laugh because she was so completely oblivious to the torture she was inflicting on the poor boy.

"I was just telling Dean he should come over for dinner sometime. What do you think?"

"That's a great idea. It's almost always just me and Mom. Sometimes Ed or Wren. I love them dearly but… it would be sooo nice to have someone closer to my own age around for a change." She turned her attention back to me. "Mom, I have to show you something. Hurry."

"Okay."

Cassie bounded off toward the kitchen and through a door that led to a garage. Dean and I followed. Lucy McBride's car had already been sold, and the smooth concrete floor was spotless. Plastic totes were stacked neatly in one corner, most labeled in the large, loopy handwriting I remembered from the blackboard as we discussed *Beowulf* and *Hamlet*. Decorations, apparently —*Halloween, Christmas, July 4ᵗʰ*. I felt a little pang of sadness that these would probably never see the light of day again. No one was going to buy someone else's memories like that. I wondered if Kenneth would throw them out or pack them up to take back to California.

The one thing that seemed out of place in the

almost obsessively tidy garage was a large cardboard box propped up against the wall next to the garage door. It looked like the kind of container that a mirror might come in—tall and wide but not very deep. Scrawled across the front in blocky letters was *Ruth Townsend—Thistlewood Star.*

"What on earth?" I said.

"Looks like she left something for you," Cassie said. "Come see. I have to confess that I already peeked."

I shook my head, laughing. "Now, why doesn't that surprise me?"

She pulled open the flap covering the end of the box. I reached in slowly to touch the frames stacked upright inside the package.

"Canvases?"

"They're paintings, Mom. Pretty good, too, based on the ones I saw."

She reached in and gently pulled the first one out.

It wasn't simply good. It was breathtaking. A large, vibrant tree took up most of the canvas. Some kind of weeping willow, maybe, but the colors were surreal. The trunk and branches were fairly normal, painted in a muddy, weathered brown acrylic. The leaves, however, were various shades of teal—some neon bright, some dark, and others almost transparent with the blue-green revealing the ugly brown below. *I'm here,* the brown seemed to say. *No matter how pretty the surface, I'm always here underneath.*

"It's beautiful," Dean said from behind my shoulder. "A little eerie, though."

I nodded. He had summed it up perfectly.

The world needs more beauty. That's what makes life worth living. Maybe this was her way of reminding me about that conversation so many years ago.

"They're *all* beautiful," Cassie said. "But why are they out here in the garage—and with your name on the box? Do you think she wanted you to have them?"

"I don't know," I said as I slid Lucy's painting back into the box. "Maybe I should go ask Kenneth."

"They'd look perfect in your office at the *Star*," Cassie said. "The place needs some color."

She was right about that. I'd been thinking for months that the office looked kind of dreary. And now that I'd taken over the newspaper, it somehow seemed right to have Lucy McBride's artwork hanging in Mr. Dealey's old office to represent the two people—well, aside from my parents—who did the most to set me on my path as a journalist.

"I think that's a good idea," I told Cassie as I rummaged in my purse to see if I'd brought my check-book. I had a little cash on me but not much, since I really hadn't expected to buy anything. For the most part, I'd come because Wren mentioned it, and I thought it would be a good opportunity to get Cassie out of the house. And looking at her just then, showing Dean the other paintings, I thought maybe that was a very good idea.

I turned to see Wren coming down the steps into the garage. "There you are! I was beginning to think y'all left me here."

"Nope. Did you get the book situation worked out?"

Wren nodded. "Twenty dollars. I feel like I'm stealing them."

"If any of those are first editions, you sort of are. And knowing Ms. McBride, that wouldn't surprise me at all."

"I know, and I tried to tell Kenneth that, but he said he's just glad to know they'll have a good home. He's out of boxes, though, so I'm going to come back later, after all of this traffic clears, and load them into the trunk. If y'all are ready to go, I'm starved. Maybe lunch at the diner? And Dean, you're more than welcome to join us."

"Wish I could," he said, "but break's over. I need to get back on my route."

"Wren, come here," Cassie said. "Ms. McBride was quite the artist. And look." She tapped my name on the box.

"I'm going back inside to talk to Kenneth," I told her. "See what he'll let them go for. My office needs a little color."

"Huh," Wren said. Her voice sounded a little strained. "I didn't know she painted. He'll probably give them to you for free, though. I had to practically shove my twenty into his hand. And if she put your name on them…"

That was true, but I wondered whether the paintings were really something her son was willing to let go. These were things his mom created with her own hands. Originals. I was pretty sure that a piece of her soul had gone into these, and that thought caused my eyes to water.

Just then, my new iPhone—a late birthday gift to myself, and unlike my old one, capable of keeping a charge for more than an hour—chirped to life in my front pocket. It was Ed Shelton, who I guess I can call my boyfriend now, although that term sounds ridiculous for a sixty-year-old man. I motioned for the others to give me a second and stepped off to the side.

"Hey, Ed. What's up?"

I listened quietly for a moment and then told him I'd be right there. Even though the garage was stifling, I shivered.

"Mom?" Cassie said. "What's wrong?"

"Lunch will have to wait. That was Ed. Someone just found a car in the river. And there's a body inside."

☆☆☆

☆ Order PALATINO FOR THE PAINTER ☆

About the Author

C. Rysa Walker is the pen name author Rysa Walker adopts when she's in the mood to tackle mysteries that are a little more grounded in reality than her various science fiction and fantasy series. Occasionally, author Caleb Amsel is her partner in crime on these adventures. Learn more about the Thistlewood Star series on Rysa's website.

www.rysa.com/mysteries

Made in the USA
San Bernardino, CA
23 December 2019